D0921591

CAST A SPELL

CAST A SPELL

◆

BETTE PESETSKY

HARCOURT BRACE & COMPANY

New York   San Diego   London

Requests for permission to make copies of any
part of the work should be mailed to:
Permissions Department, Harcourt Brace & Company,
8th Floor, Orlando, Florida 32887.

Library of Congress Cataloging-in-Publication Data
Pesetsky, Bette, 1932–
Cast a spell/Bette Pesetsky.— 1st ed.
p.   cm.
ISBN 0-15-116072-4
I. Title.
PS3566.E738C37   1993
813'.54—dc20   92-36463

Designed by Lori J. McThomas

Printed in the United States of America

First edition
A B C D E

CAST A SPELL

◆

PART I

◆

"Where are we going, Daddy?"
"You'll see. Go to sleep."
—RAUL BRANDĀO, 1908
(from "The Thief and
His Little Daughter")

G. I. Rosencantz
Sunshine Publishing Co.
Oleana, Fla. 33546–1075

Dear Mr. Rosencantz:

You may remember me from the story twenty-seven months ago called "The Reverend and the Teenage Tart." In case you don't, I enclose a clipping from your newspaper as well as a list of other places that saw fit to run that story.

I would like to propose an article—maybe in several parts. I guess I'll be straightforward about this, I intend to write an exposé about Raemunde Howard, whom you would know as Miz Magic (that TV children's show). Like all celebrities—although I am not certain that she fully qualifies there—Raemunde Howard's life cannot be above suspicion. In short—do we want *our* children to watch her?

I am prepared to devote time and effort to this. I don't expect my path to be easy. It's not as if she were a former porn star or posed nude for calendars. But I believe in the existence of secrets, Mr. Rosencantz. As my late grandmother would say: Everyone has a secret.

My credentials for this assignment are far more than evidenced by the much-syndicated story about Reverend Tounce and that child (see attached). I am Carolyn Howard, Raemunde (Miz Magic) Howard's cousin.

If you are interested, please respond quickly, as I will surely pursue other avenues for publication.

Yours,
Carolyn Howard

Carolyn Howard
Box 117
Crosby Falls, N.Y. 11172

Dear Ms. Howard:

Yes, we are interested. Certainly we do not want our children
to have as a role model anyone with a dubious past. What exactly
did you have in mind? And, Ms. Howard, are you prepared to rattle
family skeletons?

Yours truly,
G. I. Rosencantz

G. I. Rosencantz
Sunshine Publishing Co.
Oleana, Fla. 33546–1075

Dear Mr. Rosencantz:

I heard on the weather report on the late night news that
southern Florida is having some beautiful weather. I do like
warmth. Anyway, re my article about Rae (as I call her), I'll be
truthful—I am uncertain exactly where the story will take me,
but I am prepared to go as far as it does. Rae, as is known, has
had three husbands. She is currently still married to Peter. No. 3
has been in place for five years. Yes, I knew all her husbands, and
I do know that she confessed this on television—a modern American mea culpa.

But I believe that there is *more*. If I were to list what subjects
I intend to follow: sex, money, family—and the occult. This
last item came to me last night. Rae was a strange girl. Rae
is a strange woman. Does she dabble in the occult? In black
magic? I'll find out—of that you can be certain. This isn't
completely a witch-hunt—I know for a fact that Rae tells fortunes.

My cousin lives with third husband Peter, professor of cultural
sociology—God knows what that is—in Berdan. One of those up-
scale cutesy river towns (Hudson River). But—she also maintains

3

a pied-à-terre in the city. The question is—when she stays there alone, does she stay there alone?

What started me on Rae? She put this announcement in the AFL-CIO newsletters (see attached from New York issue): *"Looking for information about Nathaniel Howard last seen in Chicago on 1/10/63. Write Raemunde, Box #F312."*

Just like that I said to myself—why? Nathaniel Howard—Uncle Nat to me—is Rae's father. The date and the "last seen" tell that tale. But why now after all these years is she opening that box of *mishegoss* again? Something is up. Combine that with the fact that she is taking a year's leave from her show—a sabbatical she calls it. Rae is a genuine workaholic—one of those people to whom a vacation is anathema.

All of this, Mr. Rosencantz, leads me back to my grandmother: Everyone has a secret. As for any possible unwillingness to rattle "family skeletons"—be assured, I will be true to the art of journalism.

I would like to discuss payment, expenses, etc. Please call me (number attached).

Yours fondly,
Carrie Howard

People joked that we were triplets. Carrie and Lila and Rae. Boys sniffed at the common well of our perfume. Our inflections grew alike— the rounded *u,* the pursed *t.* People said we were the Howard sisters. But we certainly weren't. Still, we were obliged to share. The economies of life left us with one beautiful dress of gray organza that spread its net impartially across our breasts. We were flirtatious, gregarious, annoying. We had a secret language resplendent in signs, hoots, vowels. The Rae of my youth embarrassed me—why deny it? She crowded my thoughts. Lila and I are the adventurous ones—Rae is background. A party entertainer.

The psychologist Zemmler says that *orphan* is a state of mind. This, of course, is said by a man who probably grew up in a fine Georgian brick house, had a sister, a father who served in Parliament, and a mother who pleasantly volunteered to work in a soup kitchen.

Well, never mind. Orphan is a state of mind. Zemmler is right. In 1963, Rae is an orphan. My sister, Lila, and I are orphans. Ignore the fact that somewhere parents may be alive. Orphan is a state of mind. Is this the bond that holds us? The streets are full of orphans. No, it is that we share a common grandmother—the repository of our orphanness. Grandmother Minnie Howard will neither beat us nor forget to feed us. Actually, she spends most of her time staring at a photograph of herself as a bride. She thinks we don't know. We know.

Families have secrets. If the secret is great enough, it doesn't have to be kept. Such as "I Was Stalin's Mistress" or "Growing Up with Göring." It is the small secrets that must be kept. Great secrets come out all by themselves—like deathbed confessions—and are accepted, have status.

Everyone thinks that if you tell one secret, you've told all secrets. Raemunde goes on television and confesses the failure of her marriages. That was a loud secret. Quiet secrets are the most dangerous.

Listen, I didn't even know about the existence of Raemunde Howard, much less that she was a cousin. We were East Coast people. Our entire family lived in New York—maybe some migrated to Cleveland. Nothing atypical about our family. Still, people get angry. Some drift away. That's part of modern American society—this geographic severing. Raemunde Howard was born in New York City and then whisked off to Chicago, Milwaukee, St. Louis, Springfield, Champaign, and Oshkosh. My family was a clan who didn't leave New York, a covey of the ordinary who stayed—spinning, weaving, saving.

What makes our Rae famous? An absurd and trivial interest. Her obsession with magic. Carrie and Lila and Rae. We grew up together—all right, not from infancy. None of that "they slept in the same crib" crap. As if that determined life. No, we met when Rae was eleven, I was twelve, and Lila was ten. We are together and starting at square zero. But it isn't really square zero or at least not the same square. There is genetics, there is psychology, there is peer pressure. There is even chance.

I know all the details of Rae's arrival in New York. I know because she tells me. Reveals everything. Should I believe this? Absolutely. There is no reason for her to dissemble. But I hear this tale with my own child's ear. I could have missed something, ignored a clue.

Allow me to skip ahead for a moment because I do not want to forget. One year after she arrives in New York, Rae (age twelve) makes her first cape. A homemade cape of blue velvet on which she has crudely basted a constellation of silver stars of different sizes. She wears this cape to school. The cloth dips to her ankles, covers her skirt, obscures her blouse. Lila and I burn with despair. Everyone knows she is with us. On a street, in public, she wears this cape. Someone yells: "Who's the zombie?"

Does she go with empty hands? She carries this contraption. A papier-mâché copy of an Egyptian temple complete with lopsided pillars, a doll-house tin saucer, and matching teacup. "Wait until you see this," she says over and over. "This is great." In front of the entire school during assembly she displays the temple. A long metal tube is attached, a can of Sterno lit. The principle is simple—the hot air expands, water flows into the teacup, and the cup descends. What happens then? The tiny temple doors swing open. "This is magic," Rae says, and smiles at all those children. She stands there, she bows. Everyone giggles. That day, someone steals the temple from her locker.

Years later, in a fierce argument, I yell at her. "You never cry!" Rae may have noticed that to be fact, but she denies it. "Everyone cries," she says. "The people who tell you they don't cry are the same people who tell you they don't study. Born knowing the dates of the French Revolution."

In order to be systematic about this, I have subscribed to a clipping service. Bulging brown envelopes filled with paper wafers tumble into my mailbox. Who would have believed that our Rae is everywhere. Am I jealous of her? She ended up with a lot of attention. Frankly, why couldn't it have been me? That's a normal passion. Could be yours. We grew up together. Lila is attractive. I am smart. Rae—Rae is a magician. Who could have known that stupid magic could take her so far. Look at this quote from *Newsday:* "'Magic fills my needs—artistry, mystery, physical skill,' says Miz Magic. 'A magician always thinks.'"

Well, Rae was never one to hide her light under a barrel.

My plans are to run through Rae's life as I know it—and then, where there are holes, I am going to poke into them. I have sources. I know who to ask. Most important, I know what to ask.

Consider that she was married three times—this paragon of magical integrity. Just exactly how does this look to children? What kind of standards does this marital shuffle set? Sex and the magician.

Rae is a public figure—and why shouldn't the public know the truth? I'll start with the relatives—anything my memories miss, they will fill in. Listen, the first question Rae asked me was whether I had any boyfriends. I said certainly not. She said she had a few back in Chicago. I didn't believe a word of it. Later, she admitted it wasn't so.

You want to flatter anyone—call up and say you want to interview them. Doesn't matter about what. Could be about Rae. Here is Rae's story. My direct recollections. I was there.

1

If the first field of inquiry is to be sex and Rae, then it begins with Leo Littweiler—hardly an auspicious start. Leo, by the way, is not husband number one—he is number two.

Hard to believe that Rae married more than once. Our grandmother often said: What man is gonna take her on? On the other hand, Minnie and Rae weren't exactly close.

To backtrack a little, end of her junior year in high school, Lila and I fix Rae up with George Kelley. He maybe isn't a doll, but isn't all that bad. Rae doesn't have a date for Mert Levinson's party. Lila has one, I have one. We don't even draw straws—we give Rae the gray organza dress for the evening. What does she do?

George arrives.

"Pick a three-digit number," Rae says. "Don't be afraid. Pick a number."

"What? Five hundred forty-seven."

"Now," she says, "double it."

Lila moans and drags me out into the hall. "I'm going to die," she says.

"It will be all right," I say.

The evening ends at the dance—third dance. Rae pulls a cigarette from George's nose. Lila's date and mine burst into hysterical laughter. George goes out to smoke the cigarette and forgets to return.

Lila and I spend one summer trying to teach Rae how to walk. She walks like she's a parade. Not attractive in a girl.

"Watch Lila," I say.

Lila gets up and slowly, with a pronounced slouch, crosses the room. It's seductive without being a hip-swinging movement.

"I can't do that," Rae says.

"Why not, for God's sake, why not?"

"Face it—I'm not good at this. I can't do sex."

"You don't do sex—that way," Lila says. She is the one with patience. "And you certainly don't do it with magic. Even forgetting the walk, Rae, boys don't want to talk magic. Not its history, philosophy, how you practice it. They don't."

"I know," Rae says.

Leo Littweiler is not an attractive man. Frankly, he is an ugly man. He meets Rae in college. She swears that she cannot get free of him. The man is a born leech, she says. He rides with her on the subway— past his stop, his connection. Leo has a mother and a father. "I'm an orphan," Rae tells him, "and orphans are dangerous people—so get out of my face!"

Rae first saw Leo in 1970. Seven years after she arrived in New York. Leo is one of those people who likes to say that he discovered Miz Magic and her powers. You bet!

2

Rae comes to New York. I've read her interviews. She makes it sound like fun or at least like Red Riding Hood going to Grandma. How would I characterize those public admissions? Inventions, adumbrations, side trips. She can say whatever she wants—I have investigated.

Picture the future field of battle, that autumn day in 1963 when Rae Howard, with just the bitter beginning of a social services folder behind her, dreams of the unknown family in Washington Heights. A plastic tag pinned to her shirt, gives delivery data, like she is a suitcase: "Rae-munde Howard, age 11, ℅ Mrs. Minnie Howard, 8166 Carrel Place, NYC." Quite openly, Rae removes the tag before reaching Union Station.

Child Welfare in Chicago provides the escort for Rae's trip to New York. Official designation: *Abandoned Child at Risk*. They put her in the care of Charlotte DeWorth, who has a sister living in Brooklyn. A trip like this is a perk.

Mrs. Charlotte DeWorth, burdened by suitcase, reading material, handbag, decides to ignore the removal of the tag. After all, the tag only calls attention to both of them. If the rest of the world is in turmoil, neither Rae nor Mrs. DeWorth cares.

Charlotte does not like Rae. "Could be a hot number" is whispered into the woman's ear. Child Welfare had easily envisioned the growth of a thick file on Rae, despite the doctor's clean bill of health. Mrs. DeWorth cannot help wondering if growing inside Rae, in her child's womb, might be a baby. Mrs. DeWorth tries to repress the idea—after all, she has the medical report.

Child Welfare is not an agency with money to burn. They provide a bag with a toothbrush, a washcloth, and a comb. And one pair of pajamas and one set of underwear. Rae wears the clothes that she wore when first she came under official protection. Mrs. DeWorth notices that the skirt looks expensive. A red-and-blue plaid skirt of softest wool.

How long the trip is from Chicago to New York! And all the way Rae chatters on foolishly. "You're driving me crazy," Mrs. DeWorth hisses and tries a sharp pinch. "Can't you sit still?" Mrs. DeWorth doesn't want people to think this is her child. She starts a conversation with the woman across the aisle and explains the circumstances. A delivery.

Mrs. DeWorth has a food allowance, but wisely she has packed a dinner. What they do not know, they do not know. Having a reasonable appetite, she is generous. Hard-boiled eggs, ham on real rye bread—nothing in cellophane for Mrs. DeWorth—with mustard and pickles, three oranges, a small assortment of cookies. A thermos holds Mrs. DeWorth's very light coffee—almost milk and therefore could not possibly hurt the child.

But the hours drag. Rae cannot sit still. She starts an act for the amusement of her fellow travelers. Look at that kid, they say. She juggles oranges. Her sharp-edged elbows offer a ballet of arms. With disturbing agility Rae performs tricks, pulling coins from behind ears, pencils from sleeves, and, once, a dazzling paper fan created from folded comics is found behind a collar. The amused porter gives her cards. Her tricks with a deck of cards are diabolical. Is this what cardsharps do?

"Where did you learn this?" Mrs. DeWorth whispers.

"I'm a magician," Rae tells her. "Pick a card," she persuades. "This is the Hofzinser Pass. Hofzinser of Vienna. Want to see me make a card rise? I also do his floating wand, but I don't have the stuff with me."

Mrs. DeWorth wipes her face with a handkerchief. She keeps a sharp eye on the girl—especially when she is near men. Girls who have spent time—even a small amount of time—on the street create risks.

Worse yet, when the train arrives in New York, who meets them and holds up a card that says *Raemunde Howard* but a tall and angular Jew wearing a black, double-breasted suit. Mrs. DeWorth is aware that the night spent sleeping in a coach seat has rumpled her, lost her that crisp authority with which she started the journey. Still, she is torn by dark sexual visions. Should she give a child to a man? Even this particular child, whom privately she dislikes? The man says he is Minnie Howard's nephew and a lawyer. That's what he says.

Aaron Kaplinsky is extremely annoyed, sputum flies in sparks as he speaks, he waves the proper authorization and informs this idiot woman that his aunt—the child's grandmother—is sick. What does she want from him?—this low-level bureaucrat in her wrinkled dress? Bad enough that he is here. He is not good with children; he does not like children. He sees a resemblance to his cousin Nat in the girl. Or to photographs of his cousin Nat—he does not actually remember him. But what he wants—Aaron wants lunch. He would like at least a sandwich and a cup of coffee before his afternoon begins. His stomach feels sour. Why does it have to be him, anyway? His mother has tried to explain. Minnie likes you, she said. And she has the first dollar she ever made—the first dollar. Why shouldn't it go to you?

3

This is Rae's arrival in New York City. It is apparently not possible to get a copy of that report from Child Welfare. Maybe they destroyed it. At any rate, I don't believe there is any material there other than an account of Rae's abandonment. And I already know about that.

Rae in New York. No one waved a flag then. Did you see the headlines in the *New York Post* last November? "Miz Magic Comes to the Big Apple."

In the prized, large and old apartment in Washington Heights, on the very day that Rae is to arrive, life is not calm. Minnie Howard's leg has blown up. A malady that she refers to as God's revenge. Ghosts crowd around her bed. She swears that she smells them, a feral odor. The air seems to Minnie's sharp and bleating nostrils to carry a scent of private sins that deal with nakedness and phallic complications. She keeps that illusion to herself. She cannot locate a prayer for exorcism of a fancy.

She sighs, she shifts weight, she groans—unable to find a position of comfort in her bed, leg raised on a princess-high pile of feather-filled pillows. What a sight! Her hair is uncombed, her face unwashed. A glimpse of chalk-white thigh exposed. Sick, she says, is sick. Her sweat dried up years ago. For three days a practical nurse squats on a wooden chair, her presence required to offer medication, handle the bedpans.

Sometimes Minnie bellows words. "Woe is me! My life is pain." This due to the fact that life, ever unfair, destroyed the plan that Minnie carefully set up, a plan that should have kept this particular grandchild away from her forever. What happened? She fears to know. Life is torturing her.

She is a bereft mother, although memories of her children seem distant and fabricated. All the women she knows can speak fifty years later about the births they endured—how they were torn in two, how the infant looked, flat-nosed, black-haired. They remember the weight of the husband. Now Minnie is a *bubbe*. Three grandchildren—her two sons gone.

Why is she not even granted time to mourn her losses? In fact, she cannot remember the births of Laurence and Nathaniel. That comes, her sisters say, from using a modern hospital.

Carrie and Lila do not know their grandmother well. They heard that she had a falling-out with Laurence. Lila was five at the time and believes that means pushing and shoving. Carrie tells her that she is incredibly stupid.

The apartment has three large bedrooms. Carrie and Lila have been occupants for almost a year and no one has come to claim them. For a time Lila would not take her clothes out of her suit-case and dressed and undressed within its confines. Carrie shamed her. It's a room, she said, in steely tones. It's a dresser.

Before they moved in, they seldom saw Minnie Howard. They think that they last saw her at a Passover seder that ended with their father Laurence saying, "Never, never." Although what that means, they cannot know. The chair reserved for Elijah—who they believe to be a late guest—is overturned when Laurence swipes at it with his hand.

Not once in the entire year since Lila and Carrie came to live with Minnie Howard has anyone taken them to the hospital in Nyack to see their mother. Surely she worries, and so they send letters to which they receive no replies.

Minnie, accompanied by her two sisters, makes that trip to Nyack. Minnie's daughter-in-law Fay, wearing a cotton robe and with her hair cut suspiciously short, either does not know them or does not want to speak to them. Her eyes are engaged else-where.

On the way back to the city, Minnie and her sisters stop at a restaurant with a pretty view of a small pond crisscrossed by sourceless shadows, where they eat excellent plates of beef gou-lash in brown viscous gravy, potatoes in a mist of steam, and lemon cream pie for dessert. After they finish this lunch, the women agree that there is no sense in making this long ride again or dragging the girls to see this shadow of a person. Tragedy, Minnie says, is my middle name. They pile back into the gray Buick that belongs to Minnie's brother-in-law Carl.

Sensibly, they wait for further news.

In fact, no one knows what will become of Carrie and Lila. Rae has not yet arrived.

4

Appearances. We noticed right away that Rae dressed like a jerk. Like a person who didn't live in the city. First day out of the house she opens the top two buttons. That tells you something. But as for knowledge about sex at age eleven—I don't think she knew a third of what she implied. Certainly not firsthand. And I believe she was afraid of Minnie Howard.

How do I think of Minnie? I see her as a photograph. And it is amazing that the image was ever her.

This is how Minnie Howard looked. Her wedding gown had a high neckline that created for Minnie an artificially patrician neck, and the tight sleeves ended in sharp points to half-cover her hands. The total effect: medieval. Her wedding day was the most important day in Minnie's life—not because of the marriage or Gerald. No, it is because she looked so right that day, so nearly perfect. Nothing suggests the devouring future—the vindictive bosom, the hot legs with purple knots, the startling cowardices.

Minnie is sometimes embarrassed by the innocence in the eyes. But perhaps she misjudges those eyes. That she bled on her wedding day was not a miscalculation. As she told her tired husband, things happen.

She keeps her framed wedding picture on a table facing her bed. Originally that frame held a picture of her and Gerald. She put this one on top of it, slid it under the glass.

She stands alone, her sweeping train of point d'Angleterre lace draped by the photographer's assistant, whom she remembers very well. His mint-flavored breath close to her ear, then as he knelt he looked up and winked at her. Only the headdress offers historical perspective, with its crown of lace that sits straight across her forehead.

She took the photograph to Gimbel's when they had a special offer and had it colored. Her hair became a shade of honey, her lips coral, and her skin glowed with life.

Sometimes Minnie resurrects her husband, Gerald, in her mind—dead twenty-two years—and ages him along the lines of the husbands of her friends. Thus, he sits at her table with thickened waistline, with hair nearly gone, and he tells her how things are in the fittings business. Things are lousy.

If Gerald had not died, life would not have been different. She does not express that thought—it would be misunderstood. But it is true. She remembers when Gerald went into the Army. She thought of herself as an Army wife and regularly attended meetings of the Red Cross. But otherwise, and she was amazed, she really didn't notice his absence.

When Gerald died, it was six o'clock in the morning. He had been on his way to open the factory. He clutched to his chest a thermos of coffee. The street empty. Empty, Minnie says afterward. One car coming down the street. When she gets the call, Gerald is already dead. Her brother-in-law Carl goes to the hospital for his clothes, his wallet, his keys. She is told not to go, not to look.

Minnie does not really remember Gerald. She does not think that her sons do, either. He has become such a blur that having his picture in front of her is like staring at a stranger. She prefers the other picture—the one of her alone.

5

Aaron is the one who delivers Rae to her grandmother. In the taxi, Aaron doesn't speak to Rae, and she doesn't speak to him. She looks out the window. Neither minds. No one asks her who she is and so she cannot say that she is a magician.

Rae is not frightened. By her wits, she has escaped several possible fates. She believes that if her father is somewhere—and why shouldn't he be somewhere?—then eventually he will come and get her. It doesn't matter where she is, he'll find her. This is a common belief held by all abandoned children—no matter the reason. Carrie and Lila believe that their mother will get well and rescue them. Even when they scoff and deny—they believe.

Aaron leaves Rae in the hall. Don't touch anything, he admonishes. But what would she touch? The apartment is burdened with furniture. A parade of mahogany. Who wants anything here? She hums, she exercises her fingers. The unlikable Aaron trots down the length of the hallway. He is replaced by the nurse who sighs and smiles and nods.

The nurse feels sorry for Rae. She knows the entire story. Minnie Howard spends the day talking on the telephone. This is the illegitimate child. The nurse knows that a lot of people don't think this way anymore. But she does. Minnie Howard regards the nurse as if she is a piece of furniture. As if she is deaf. As if she doesn't matter.

The nurse gossips wearily about her cases. She told her newest boyfriend about this one. A ball breaker, she says, and I pity the new kid coming. The old woman will sit on her.

The nurse rummages in the pocket of her sweater for something sweet. Nature has given her one pleasure: She may eat all the candy she wishes and not a pound grows on her frame. The nurse would give Rae a candy, but beneath the tissue there is only one small chocolate left, and the afternoon is long. So the nurse sighs.

Everyone in this house calls her nurse, even the little girls. That part she likes. Sometimes people take advantage of LPNs. She hates it when they look at her name tag and call her Edie and ask her if she wouldn't mind touching up a collar or two. Just while the patient naps.

At last it is Rae's turn to meet Minnie Howard. No one takes her by the hand or says my dear child. Aaron motions her onward and the nurse waves. Rae goes into the bedroom.

Imagine the first sight of Minnie in that rumpled bed, half seen behind an escarpment of pillows. So Rae puts on her best winsome smile. The one she used with the hidden cabinet trick. Rae, the only child of Nathaniel Howard. Paternity undeniable. Note the bony cheeks, the lilac-blue eyes, the loping gait. The widow's peak. Rae is an example of what is meant when they say—oh, she is her father's daughter.

Minnie Howard's eyes are red-ringed and moist. She is a crier, a pitiless weeper. She brays at God and condemns His actions.

These are not tears for Rae. If Rae wants tears, let her cry herself. Minnie sobs for the scandals that life grants her. Life has given her only these leavings from what she considers to have been her fruit.

Minnie Howard isn't as old as Rae thought. People always expect grandmothers to be older. Rae had imagined a tall woman, a ruler of sorts. Instead, here is this person with bare patches on her head and smelling of moderate decay.

For a moment, life is not yet set, and Rae can be optimistic. This is her grandmother. Perhaps Rae has a conception of this relationship based on hearsay or culled from books.

Rae steadies the smile and glides over to the bed. She is glad that she is wearing short sleeves. More effective that way. She holds out her hands and displays those empty palms. Turns her hands over. What's the principle? Nothing up your sleeve.

Her fingers are properly flexed, natural in appearance. She leans forward toward Minnie. Her right arm extends; hand carefully in view, the fingers brush those spikes of gray hair and artfully extract a quarter from behind Minnie's ear. Rae tosses the coin in the air and catches it heads up.

"That's mine," Minnie Howard says. "You little thief!"

6

You have to understand—we were there first. Carrie and Lila. Maybe it wasn't a scene from Dickens, but we were orphans. That was in a way a distinction. They're orphans, our grandmother used to say. They have no one. Sometimes Minnie referred to us as the bitter leavings of her fruit.

Carrie and Lila are sisters. They fret and are noisy. During meals they deliberately swing their shoes against the mahogany table legs. They have an elaborate point system for evaluating nicks. Carrie believes that they might have been adopted. Their parents—particularly the mother—could be anyone. Maybe Ida Lupino or Loretta Young. She hunts for papers, for evidence in Minnie Howard's house, but finds nothing.

Carrie divides up the shared bedroom. Keep your baby things over there, she tells Lila. The nights in that apartment are fearsome. Carrie, who used to tattle regularly, now says nothing when Lila cries in the night for her mother.

Minnie from her bed conducts a mental survey of the apartment. Her sons—may they rest in peace (one for sure)—lived together in relative harmony in the room occupied now by the legitimate Carrie and her sister, Lila. The third bedroom was always prepared, always ready, its linen untouched. It is the company bedroom. Why use it now?

Minnie says that Rae should be very comfortable in the room off the kitchen. The apartment was designed for better days. Minnie has never had a live-in maid. She has cleaning women who come by the day and exasperate her and are discharged regularly.

Carrie tells her friends about this arrangement. One of the girls repeats this to her mother, who says it reminds her of an old Shirley Temple movie except she thinks Shirley was put into an attic bedroom.

7

It is the LPN who tells Minnie that the child—the new child—comes with nothing. No suitcase. She has only the small bag filled with the provisions from Child Welfare. The nurse enjoys that.

Minnie hits her forehead weakly—she is put upon still again. And she sees that Rae is too big to share Carrie's clothes. Rae is younger but taller.

For many years Minnie has successfully kept her son Nat from her thoughts. He just wasn't. Now, the girl is made in his image. Minnie remembers the mother. Oh, too well she recalls Celia Claire. A small girl with ropes of silky hair. She had not married Nat. They lived together and it was known that he would have married her. But Rae does not look like Celia Claire. She might have been a one-parent child.

Minnie talks on the telephone, one after another she tells her sisters about this misfortune. The child is virtually bare, has come with enormous needs. Minnie is hoping that, considering the state of her leg and her health, one or another of them might offer to help. In the end, they all gave the same suggestion: Why not send that woman out shopping—the nurse—with the child, of course. After all, you're paying her mainly to sit. Send them out to buy a few things. To get by.

So armed with twenty-five dollars, LPN Edie finds herself walking the two blocks to the stores. Rae is with her. Edie has been told to go to Zwelner's—a store that she knows. A store renowned for its low prices and the sad quality of its goods. Edie feels badly treated. She will arrange the purchases to allow enough for a chocolate soda. She looks down at the little girl who says nothing. No, she will arrange the purchases for two sodas. Someone should light a candle for that child.

Years later, the nurse recognizes Rae on television. "I knew her when she was a kid," she tells her husband—for by now she is married. "You did not," he says. "You don't know anybody on television."

8

Carrie and Lila do not want another cousin. They have been given no time to mourn their own losses. Attempts at moping are not encouraged. Already, bits and pieces of who they are fade. The hold of the past is never completely firm. They consider their condition temporary. (Zemmler deals with this in his treatise "Orphans of the Moment.")

Carrie and Lila still believe home is an apartment in New Rochelle, where if you plaster your forehead to the left living-room window and stare at the farthest corner, the waters of the Long Island Sound appear in the shape of a distinct triangle. The rooms have windows and sunlight, and for a brief time they have a cat named Martha. When Lila starts to wheeze and sniffle, the cat is sent away. Which is part of the reason why Carrie does not like her sister. The girls always shared a room, but that room—the one in New Rochelle—seems to them to be bigger (not true).

They remember their mother better than they remember their father. Actually, Lila doesn't remember him at all. Except that he made her cry. Her father had stiff order books with dozens of attached carbons. He was furious, and Lila was loudly scolded for drawing on page after page of one of these notebooks—ruining something called consecutive numbers. In Lila's memory, this incident achieves the permanence of family lore.

Carrie, years later, is surprised to learn that her father didn't travel. She always thinks of him as someone who roamed unknown cities—small and sad cities.

Carrie and Lila attend a school that they think of as much worse than their previous school (not true). They know that this new cousin will probably go to this school with them, that she will sit at the table in Minnie's apartment and eat with them—what else they cannot imagine.

The girls do not know how Rae will fit in where they are. Carrie thinks of herself as strong, brave, smart. She inherited her mother's good complexion and nothing, she believes, from Laurence. Lila is small and weepy—but even that fulfills a role.

Rae is this complete unknown. For that reason, Carrie and Lila prepare to dislike her. It occurs to Carrie that life is not fair, because if they don't like Rae they cannot send her away to follow the cat Martha.

Carrie makes a list of what she expects: Rae is to watch only those television shows that she (Carrie) selects; Rae is not to take the biggest piece of anything; Rae is not to remove anything from the room that she (Carrie) shares with Lila without prior permission.

When Carrie and Lila come home from school that Thursday, Rae has packages sliding from her arms to the couch—clearly, her packages. A suspicious shadow of chocolate near her upper lip. And her skirt, Carrie realizes, is quite nice.

Rae speaks first. "I'm Raemunde Howard."

"I'm Carrie Howard."

"I'm Lila Howard."

They stare at each other. The packages are between them. Lila, who sings when she is nervous, begins a tuneless but loud chant and rubs fevered hands. *Um, lum, um, lum* bubbles forth. As the chant grows, it inspires a fierce typhoon of pounding on the headboard of Minnie Howard's bed—somewhat sparing the neighbors below. Rae and Carrie and Lila. They are united. There is a common enemy.

Carrie and Lila and Rae spend their first evening together. Carrie and Lila think of Minnie as their grandmother only—you can feel possessive even of what you don't like.

Carrie knows everything about the building, the peculiarities, the many turns of the basement, the storage of trash. That the slimy wrinkled man who lives next door is almost deaf. That is a great advantage. Three other children live in the building—they are toads. All the other families have been here for decades. They stay in and grow old. They cannot bear the thought of those huge rooms with architectural bits—the wainscoting, the carved mantel, the broken-winged seraphim—belonging to anyone else. Even the super does not go. The super's name is Pearson. He has an ulcer and drinks chalk-white medicine and quarts of milk and moans about better days. What are better days? Mr. Mableby from the fourth floor goes to the basement one afternoon. Fearful of rats and remembering tales about roaches as big as cats, he pokes into what once was a storage room.

There—he tells everyone the next day—in the darkest corner, piles of canvas awnings brutally molded, nested, frayed. Carrie says she watches Mr. Mableby and that every Saturday he goes into apartment 5C. An Indian family lives there. The man works for Transit. Mr. Mableby walks into 5C at ten o'clock in the morning and leaves exactly one hour and fifteen minutes later. How can he stand her? Carrie says. Her hair stinks of cooking oil. You can bet, Carrie says, that he is not after curry.

No one in the building is allowed to have a dog or even a bird, if you observe the fine points. But there are birds. Two parakeets live on nine. The parrot on five is half blind, but still requires care on approach—otherwise he will bite your finger. He took off the tip of the right ring finger of Mrs. Orkin, who owns him.

Lila says that she was supposed to take dancing lessons this year. Her mother promised. Grandmother Howard will not pay for them. She says that she paid for piano lessons for her own sons and look where that got them.

9

No one knows that these girls will love and not love the same men. And in the end they will untangle themselves and go with men whom the others do not know. They believe in true love. They commit to this love under the usual terms of for better or worse.

But now Rae invites her cousins into her room, the mean status of which she quickly observed. However, she dances into the room that opens directly off the kitchen and opposite the broom closet. Look, she says, isn't it cozy? So light and airy. She displays the charm of that room—and for the first time Carrie and Lila notice that its single window faces the back, where a field of rubble doesn't hide the sun. It is the brightest room in the house, featuring a hazy blue sky. And perhaps the warmest. For they have already noticed that the heat leaves the kitchen last. Yes, it is a cunning room. The furniture painted glossy white.

And that is where they will spend their evenings, creeping back to their own room only to sleep.

On that first night, they sit cross-legged in a row on Rae's bed, with its shiny white headboard. They eat peanut butter smeared on packaged chocolate-chip cookies. Licensed PN Edie brought those cookies back from her shopping expedition with Rae. She hid them in a cupboard. Rae saw her. The girls miss two television shows that Carrie loves. She forgets.

Lila says that when her mother comes home—certainly by June—she and Carrie will return to New Rochelle to live.

Carrie gets a secretive look in her eyes. "My mother," she says softly, "used to kiss a man who owned a shoe store." "Did not," Lila says. "Oh yes," Carrie says. "And you do remember we bought shoes from him. Your red sneakers and my blue. The man had a great mustache," Carrie says. "Very romantic."

Only one of the men whom they are later to know well can be described in this way. And he didn't last. Sometimes they think that they were cheated of romance.

Carrie and Lila have lived only two places in their lives. In New Rochelle and here. Rae cannot truly remember where she has lived—not every single place. Where is home? Carrie says, without hesitating: New Rochelle in apartment F17. If she repeats that, Lila will cry.

Rae finds out what they do know about her. Nothing recent. She realizes with pride that she is like a legend in the family. It is what her stepmother, Smyrna, always said: Hanky-panky widens the eyes.

10

Right after Rae arrives, her life history comes up. It is a huge history to which I paid plenty of attention. Every family has such stories, borrowed from a lifetime of difficulty. I could, one of the aunts says, fill an encyclopedia. But these stories are not for outsiders—in the family is one thing, but not other ears.

She is a bastard. That I heard first from LPN Edie. It appears that the entire family knows how Rae's mother (Celia Claire) packed a suitcase one morning, left the baby with a neighbor, and went off. Like that, they say. Like that.

Consider this! We are speaking about a middle-class young woman, not poor. How often did she go off and abandon the infant?

Who would believe that Celia Claire could vanish so completely? She didn't follow the customs of the period—no commune, no flower child. Someone says that a record exists that she went briefly to Yugoslavia, but that could be apocryphal. She was once even supposedly sighted on a train in Liverpool. All this reiterated as fact, including implications of death—suicide—and other crimes.

A baby requires a mother. Can a baby be bounced from relative to relative? For how long? A colicky baby, a rash-embroidered baby, a baby who smells from the wrong diet.

A marriage is arranged just like that—one-two-three—between Nat and the Polish girl, Smyrna, who is perhaps, just perhaps, a cousin. She is more than Polish—she is foreign. And the family knows.

Minnie is surely cursed—she has Rae, twice abandoned, ending up at her doorstep. And Minnie's sisters—who know the shape of Minnie's brassiere, the pressures of her stomach, the insides of every cupboard in her kitchen—would not believe that they do not know everything. Didn't they just hear that Rae Howard arrived without a drop of clothes? Carrying only a plastic bag no bigger than the one that holds a loaf of bread.

For a long time I thought Minnie's strange behavior was the point— you know, the take-off point for my search. I remember Minnie being unusually quiet after Rae arrived. Was she telling her sisters less? The details, for instance. The how and why.

I swear I overheard a conversation about a letter from Child Welfare and a telephone call. But this conversation was actually between Minnie and Minnie. Mumblings, indistinct. There must have been something that she couldn't confess. But what?

Minnie's sisters believe that this new reticence is due to the act of abandonment—how many children are abandoned *twice?* Was it the condition of Rae? Her physical appearance, possibly diseased—certain horrible maladies exist in the world. Illnesses that they could not immediately identify.

That is what they think—because what else could it be?

It will be Minnie who first discovers that Rae is a magician. Is it dangerous? Children play games. But then they should stop. This child could be the death of her. Minnie wishes that she was more religious, so she would know what to do. There must be a prayer for casting out heathenish thoughts—from Rae.

Minnie vaguely remembers her mother spitting in the direction of a certain woman. *Klipeh!,* her mother said. Something also was done with vinegar and onions, but Minnie hadn't watched.

If there was a secret, it's amazing that Minnie kept it. As far as I know, she never kept another. Didn't she tell her sisters when Celia Claire was pregnant? Although her son Nat swore her to secrecy—still she tells her sisters. When Laurence, uncharacteristically drunk and tired and distraught, comes to her and says how he wishes, oh, how he wishes, that he could get a divorce and start his life anew somewhere, even though he loves his wife and daughters—he really does—that, too, Minnie tells.

11

For a while, it seemed as if this could be the time and spot. I searched through all of Minnie's papers. I must say she kept a poor written record—no philosophy, no plans, no greetings. Largely fiscal debris. So I never found anything—no notes or letters about Rae.

Then, I thought it through. No, this early period in Rae's life is not significant. After all, she is only eleven years old when she appears— dropped like a moth by Child Welfare. She recites her life to us. She has no heavy experience. The narrative is: Rae is abandoned. Minnie can't face it—never mind the stepmother (after all, Rae isn't her flesh), but Nathaniel is the father. The reticence is simply family pride and annoyance. Rae was never supposed to return. The forgotten infant metamorphosing into this child. Too much! On this subject Minnie is never heard to speak.

12

Minnie Howard lives in this six-room apartment in Washington Heights, its threshold first crossed as a bride. Rae is once heard to say, Don't you East Coast people ever move?

It is an apartment barricaded against sunlight; its windows gaze down on the square courtyard of dust and up into the windows of the building's opposite wing. Old tenants say that you should have seen the building when it was new. Fabled breezes in the courtyard. Green-and-white-striped cloth awnings every summer and real plants in the lobby, fringes of ivy.

When Minnie is a bride, her mother-in-law takes her to a furniture store. Buy, she orders, firmly clutching an arm, for tomorrow. Buy to last. Awesomely heavy cabinets are ordered, a table with four leaves for a room that couldn't accommodate one. A bookcase that will hold china figurines and a silver samovar after Gerald dies. Oriental rugs over pads of jute. A dizzying number of chairs and pillows. Machine-stitched lace runners, with patterns like hex signs.

These are the rooms where they brought Carrie and Lila. And later, Rae. Minnie Howard sits in her sister Ida's kitchen and bemoans her fate. Two sons she raised—neat as pins, those boys. Now she has girls like hoydens, who would surely be the death of her. She has lost her beloved sons and acquired their offspring—two girls and a *momzer*. For emphasis she grabs a serving spoon from the draining basket and hits her breast, and her sister restrains her from doing bodily harm to herself.

The *momzer* is Rae—bastard grandchild come home to roost.

Now, it is possible that Rae could have ended up elsewhere. She never believes that every event is ordained. All sorts of choices exist. She used to say that she could have gone at age eleven to Detroit and had another life. She used to imagine that she had gone to Detroit and lived there and had two children and found herself performing as a magician at children's parties. And it is even possible that she would have left that life in Detroit and one day found herself in the river town of Berdan, sitting in a railroad station pretending to read, shivering, and heading for the city on a Monday.

13

Count up our tragedies as we might, nothing in our lives matches those belonging to Rae. Lila says that isn't so. But that's the therapist talking. Our tragedies were ordinary—the dead father and the sick mother. Rae had it all—abandonment by the mother, abandonment by the father—and, in between, some kook of a stepmother. Rae likes her—the stepmother, Smyrna. Probably because she was easy on her. Lila says that the woman's lack of care and concern is reflected in Rae's behavior. Chances are that Rae's first sexual knowledge or awareness came from this Smyrna woman.

When Lila became a therapist, she learned about the importance of the First Six Years. They make you, she says and believes that explains Rae.

Rae is never heard to blame Smyrna for anything that happened. Forget any Cinderella and the wicked stepmother tales. Rae is careful. She will not mention Smyrna's name for a long time. She remembers how Child Welfare kept prying: Smyrna's whereabouts, her last name. Some people mix into everything.

This Smyrna is Rae's main source of information about her *real* mother, Celia Claire. She says Rae's mother had a tiny waist and wore pointy brassieres. I saw her once, just once, Smyrna says. Stuck-up. Looks at me like I was pure glass. Well, my fine Miss Nothing—I'd love to see you today! Who's sleeping with Nat now?

Smyrna never tells a complete story. Bits and pieces you have to grab quick before they fade from her thoughts. Like how Rae was born. Under the circumstances, of course, some facts may have altered. Rae was born in New York City in 1952 in the unhallowed bed located in a room above The Real Nice Cleaners on Lenox Avenue where it crosses One Hundred and Twenty-first Street. For this life, Nat breaks Minnie's heart over and over. Minnie tells the family that even for the baby they won't marry. The mother and father. A *shanda*—God forbid the neighbors find out!

Once Smyrna says to Rae, You'll never guess what she left in that apartment. You'll never guess what she left, your mother. Moved out and left behind a sweater. A blue cashmere sweater, like new. You know what I did? I threw it out!

Is Smyrna the daughter she claims to be? You should have seen me, Smyrna says. I had no one in the world. And they—my dead mother's family—do you think they wanted me? But they took me anyway. The International Red Cross sent a letter.

The old uncle, Joseph, remembers the name—Dubroshna Kapaelinski. That he remembers from a photograph and translations of letters. The photograph, one of those thick cracked-looking cardboard ones, was of his father, age thirteen, and his father's sister, now dead, and another girl, whom his father said was a cousin. The names were written on the back of the picture in the popular spidery handwriting of the time. The other girl was Dubroshna. She is dead, said the International Red Cross. It is her daughter who wants to come to New York. Not a child—an adult woman.

The first words Minnie Howard says are "Why would anyone have stayed in Cracow after the war? Who in her right mind—tell me that? Look at the years gone by. Doesn't she realize it is 1952?"

The old man, Joseph, is less belligerent. "We don't know," he says. "Who are we to know?"

Poor Smyrna. They wait for her in an apartment in the Bronx at a family "introduction" dinner. All evening—as the trays of boiled brisket, of noodle pudding, of sharply spiced garlic pickles pass from hand to hand—the eyes are on her. How had she survived? They want to know. Tell us. "It was hard," Smyrna says. "Times were hard."

That, the women whisper in the kitchen. Only that she says. Hard could mean anything. Hard could mean anything from not enough coffee to horrors. Which was it?

And how could she be the daughter of Dubroshna? Dubroshna, according to memory, had been a short and dumpy woman with a strangely squash-shaped head. This one—her child—is a strapping girl, nearly six feet tall, with sparse although real blonde hair and long sturdy legs. If she was Dubroshna's daughter—then who was the father?

The bosoms heave. Spoons wave and globs of mayonnaise

dangerously fly. Minnie Howard has the loudest voice: "Why has Smyrna studied English? Why, if not to come to America and live off us? That girl has a plan. That is why."

Could you blame them?

No one is certain who has the original idea. Everyone says it is a good deal. After all, Nat is a man who travels. He is a union man, an organizer. He doesn't have a dime to his name. Where is he going to find a mother for that baby? Answer that, they say. Minnie is the holdout. There are plenty of decent girls, Minnie tells her son. Move your butt! You don't need this Polish *shiksa.*

Nevertheless, Nat asks Smyrna to marry him. Speed is necessary, he explains, because he is being transferred to Chicago. He goes where the union needs him. Yes, she would marry him— this fast.

Minnie mourns out loud. It is what she expected. Anyone could see right from the start how that girl set her cap for Nat.

And as for him—well, she expects that, too. Her son is a disappointment, a weakness, an aberration—his accomplishments not the subject of bragging. He is nothing in a family of doctors, lawyers, four accountants.

One of the aunts, the sister of Minnie's dead husband, Gerald, relents—her heart is soft and she sobs in movies. She would hold a buffet for the couple in her own home. A small buffet. And that, she says, is that.

What would it hurt if each guest brought a casserole? A favorite dish? The women are proud of their cooking. The food ultimately would be the best at any wedding remembered: stuffed breast of veal, meatballs in puddles of black gravy, pâtés of fish, red cabbage stunningly spiced, roast duck liver, salmon tartare. The china is stamped Made in Poland on the bottom of each plate, and the rims are embellished with a decoration of cornucopias of unnaturally bright fruit. The wineglasses, lent by a cousin for the affair, are prized for their heft, their carvings of diamonds and hexagons. The Sblinskis call at the last moment and donate the cake. The cake arrives in the Sblinskis' own white delivery van. Six tiers. How ostentatiously huge—becoming in the living room a focal point, as if it were a fireplace. A pillar of a cake! The suspicion is that the cake is meant for a wedding that had jumped the tracks. Still, on the top, in creamy pink icing in letters spun from a tube, it says: Nathaniel and Smyrna.

14

You know what I remember most? Rae practicing. She practiced that magic of hers like a nut. She was a pain. Friends avoided her. Pick a card, Rae would say. Watch this. I remember getting up once, it was maybe four in the morning. Rae was in the kitchen in her pajamas. The light on over the sink. She had this glass of water filled to the brim and an egg. She saw me and smiled. "You'll never guess," she says. "You bet I won't," I say. I went back to bed. That was Rae. Try living with that for years.

In the evenings after Minnie Howard limps off to bed, Carrie and Lila and Rae sit in the bedroom off the kitchen, where it is safe to talk. Carrie is now fifteen, Lila is thirteen, and Rae is fourteen. Carrie has been felt up in the movies; she pronounces it not as much fun as she thought. Lila, though, is the first asked. She feels no urges and allows no liberties. Still, she is asked. She looks as if secrets are in her, and her lower lip has acquired a trembling twitch. It is irresistible.

"I want to be something," Carrie declares. "Be something, be something." She lists her major interest in school as "undecided."

"What?" Lila asks, but does not care. She is going to be a nurse. Her friend Ginny received a nurse kit three years ago. Lila is allowed free access to it—this play is done behind closed doors; they are too old for such play. Ginny does not care about being a nurse; she yearns to be a patient.

"I'll know when the time is right," Carrie says. She feels artistic—she moves freely in the arts.

"You'll have to settle," Rae says. "Otherwise you can't be anything."

"That's stupid—I can be many things. And you—for God's sake, do you want to pull rabbits out of a hat all your life?"

"Magic is a way of life."

"Oh, really. You mean you dream of being a dreary little magician forever, doing the Rotary or Hadassah or junk like that."

"I can invent new magic, I can perfect the old—there's a lot. For instance, I would like to prove the impossibility of Houdini sending a code message back from the grave."

"All I can say is that sometimes you're a joke, Rae, do you know that? Sometimes, the kids—the other kids—think you're a joke."

"You should just be a fortune-teller," Lila says. "That's where the money is."

Rae could have gone at age eleven to Detroit and had another life. She used to imagine that she had gone to Detroit and lived there and had two children and found herself performing as a magician at children's parties. And it was even possible that she would have left that life in Detroit and one day found herself in the river town of Berdan, sitting in a railroad station, pretending to read, shivering for what was to come, and heading for the city on a Monday.

15

Carrie and Lila and Rae all have long, rebellious-adolescent hair. They have Howard hair, their grandmother says. Hair neither smooth nor neat, and difficult to style. Rae's friend Leo knew them all when they were young girls. He makes the comment that Carrie so loves and repeats to her image in the mirror. "You have voluptuous hair," Leo says. "I have never seen such voluptuous hair."

They wouldn't cut their hair—let Minnie threaten all she wants. They grow their hair wildly long and part on the left side. That makes them resemble each other—a common belief is that they are sisters. Carrie is strong. Lila is pretty. Rae has etched and gaunt features. To their grandmother, they don't look alike at all.

Minnie warns them against the accidents of rape, against dark streets, against permitting man or boy to lean against them when the bus sways.

Lila is the first one of us to inquire about birth control. That is no surprise. Right from first grade—even before Rae came—Lila was attracting boys. It is as if she sprang from the womb full of social graces. Anyway, she's the one who finds this Dr. Havering. He'll do it without parental consent. What we need is money, she says.

Rae has the money. It isn't a loan. She has it—we use it. All three of us go to this man's office. Lila swears that it isn't seedy, frightening, sinful. She is right. Only a ground-floor office in an apartment right off Mosholu Parkway. In the waiting room, perfectly respectable people. Myopic, fat mothers, snot-dribbling kids. An old man with a distinct urine odor. We sit there—three teenage girls. One of the mothers asks, "What for?"

Lila smiles. "Shots," she says.

Now this money that Rae has. From a fortune-telling performance at a fund-raiser at St. Clarence and from another at the UJA Regional. No implication that Rae isn't generous. But this year from my journalistic endeavors I made five thousand dollars. I don't have to live on this— my husband has a salary. But the point is I work hard, and for what? Five thousand dollars.

This year—God knows how much Rae made!

G. I. Rosencantz
Sunshine Publishing Co.
Oleana, Fla. 33546—1075

Dear G. I.:

I guess your initials got you plenty of ribbing. People never consider when they name kids. Don't think it was easy on Rae-munde Howard when anyone found out what Rae was short for.

Anyway, this (see attached) is what I remember personally about Rae's girlhood. Takes us up to age 17 or 18. Don't despair—I haven't had the relatives' interviews transcribed yet.

My expenses to date: Listed by interview. Some useful relatives are dead. I admit to being picky. Who wants to hear from a *dray-kop?*

Interview with Aunt Ida Loberg (Minnie Howard's last living sister) Cab fare to and from (her neighborhood isn't what it used to be, so I avoided the subway)— $9.40 (receipts attached). Three microtapes for Dictaphone AS504— $7.35 (receipts attached—to be used for more than this interview).

Interview with Dr. Lila Howard (my sister, Rae's cousin) Subway— $2.50 (no receipts)
Lunch—(Sebastian Seafood) $34.75. (If you want Lila to talk, you have to feed her. Period.) (receipt attached)

I'll be honest—I don't know if I got from either of these interviews what I wanted. Maybe the relatives misremembered. Maybe they censored their memories.

Sincerely,
Carrie Howard

G. I. Rosencantz
Sunshine Publishing Co.
Oleana, Fla. 33546 – 1075

Dear G. I.:

I enclose the unedited transcripts of the interviews with Aunt Ida and my sister, Lila. Perhaps you need them for your records.

As ever,
Carrie Howard

Ida Loberg

She is my dead father's aunt. My great-aunt. How close a relationship is that? The truth is that I do not really know Ida Loberg. Forget she was a steady companion to my grandmother's refrigerator. I saw her as an annoyance. She gave terrible advice. But know her? I probably didn't. You can gather that I have trouble locating her. Wait a few years in any family and, suddenly, where are the people? Who moved? Who died? Lila has an old address. Not there. Then I call our cousin Debbie—a second or third cousin—who lives in Bronxville. Long time no see, I say. Well, I found out she has an address, because once in a while she hears from Ida's son Max. Debbie says I couldn't call direct, because Ida doesn't have a telephone, but her neighbor does. This is a shock—the Ida I knew lived for the telephone. Still, I found her.

Ida Loberg lives in a three-room apartment off the Grand Concourse in the Bronx. What a dirty building. Depressing. Even the graffiti is uninteresting. Her apartment—what happened to all her furniture? Nothing matches. Ida was always one for sets, a world by twos—lamps, figurines, tables. This is from the time when she used to live on Long Island in Bellport in one of those mother-daughter houses. Debbie says after Ida's husband, Carl, got emphysema and sold his appliance store, they moved back to the city to be near Montefiore Hospital. Carl, Debbie thinks, is in a nursing home on Allerton Avenue.

I set up the appointment.

Ida is a flabby woman, a lumpy woman. She is what you don't want old age to do to you—moles with black hairs, cartoon circles of rouge. For contrast, look at the photograph taken of her in 1937. I know youth is temporary—everyone knows that. But see her at twenty—fierce, determined, even in the picture she looks as if she is moving, except for the eyes locked in a frozen gaze.

This is our conversation.

Ida: Well, well, look who's here—one of the fine younger members of the family. Come to visit an old woman, eh? Pig's eye—Come in Carolyn. If you stand in the doorway—you think I don't know where I live?—you get mugged. Oh, pardon me—it's Carrie, not Carolyn, Carrie.

Well, Carrie—a better future for you than Sister Carrie. Didn't know I read Dreiser. No, sirree. Look at an old lady, varicose veins bigger than both legs put together and nothing that doesn't sway. Right away assume the owner is a *dummkopf.* I went one semester to City before I got married. My mother said without marriage you might as well be dead.

When did I last see you? God knows—and that's the truth. I ever see you since Minnie died? So now, out of the blue—like a shot from heaven—I get a telephone call from the younger generation. What do I know about our Rae? She's everywhere, that girl. Who would have believed it?

I go to the laundromat. I talk to total strangers—a lot of nice black ladies in the neighborhood. They see Rae's picture everywhere—she's selling something on TV, she's on a T-shirt. My grandniece, I say. My sister—may she rest in peace—her granddaughter.

Raemunde Howard. Miz Magic. Rae. I could shake my head a dozen times when I think about that. If we took a vote about all the girls in the family—and I include the dentist's two—Rae would come in last. How to succeed? Her mother was—what did they call them?—a free spirit. What I think—and do not repeat this—is that she was a communist. She dressed like Greta Garbo in that movie. All tweedy. And la-de-dah.

The first time I saw Raemunde Howard was on November 22, 1963. The day Kennedy was shot. How do I know? The televisions are blaring so much—I could hardly think. I come over to Minnie's apartment. We had a little bit of an argument—over what? The year Myron Cohen played in *Orphans' Storm.* Never mind. She was wrong. It was 1946.

"So stranger," Minnie says.

I am not looking at her. I am looking across the room. Sitting in a chair is this skinny, bony girl. With, frankly, her father's face. Her father's daughter—and Nat could have been found in the bulrushes for all he acted like a son. A thousand times I told my sister, sometimes blood is water. I'm no stranger to that.

When my Max's marriage broke up—you know he went off with a singer. From a group—The Singing Sirens. He isn't gone six weeks when his wife—his former wife—upchucks us. Carl wheezing and can hardly breathe. Selling the house, she says. So here we are—here I am.

But Rae. That one.

"My God," I say to Minnie. "It's like looking at Nathaniel. If he had been born a girl."

"You saw Rae before," she says.

Now she knows I haven't.

"Rae," Minnie calls, "stop the nonsense, stop that *mishegoss,* and come here. This is like an aunt to you—Aunt Ida."

I was walking at that time with a cane—a beautiful cane from Majorca, with ivory triangles set in the handle. Gone. One day a kid snatched that cane—bet he got ten dollars for it. But I had it then, placed it by my chair.

Rae comes over, she smiles, she holds out her hand. I thought it was going to be a shake. Not for a second. She takes the cane, kind of feels it in her hand. Boom—next thing it's hanging in the air. Not one of her fingers were bent over it. She does some fancy steps—a Fred Astaire. The cane is floating.

"Am I an *alrightnik,* Auntie," she says, "or am I not?"

(Comment: Rae showed Lila and me how you do that. It's a matter of finding the balance point for the cane and then supporting that spot on the fatty part of your palm. I'm not saying it's easy, but it's possible.)

"The idiot!" Minnie says. "Magic, magic, magic. Thinks she's going to become a magician. Like that was something for a girl."

"Not going to be a magician—am a magician," Rae says. "Keep watching."

Minnie slaps her own forehead. "That's what she does," she says. "She'll be the death of me. All day she does this—one trick after another." She reaches out—but it is like trying to catch a fish without a hook. "Put that down!" Minnie screams.

Rae shrugs, she puts the cane on my lap, bows, exits.

"What was that?" I say. I examine the cane—it looks all right.

"She comes with a curse," Minnie says. "Better she should bite her fingernails—that I could paint with iodine. That was magic."

"So what does she have—one of those magic kits? And what's so terrible—Max collects baseball cards and Elaine's little girl does something-or-other."

"This one doesn't stop," Minnie says.

I was stupid—I didn't realize what this was doing to Minnie. Rae should have been slapped down hard. If she had been in my house. One more trick, I would have said, and I'll show you what to watch—Miss Know It All.

I didn't understand. I figured kid's stuff. Later, to be honest, I thought, maybe, of a *dybbuk.* But did I consider that there was a future in this? I never.

One day, I think Minnie has had enough. "Tell me," I ask, "is she here for good?"

"God has it in for me, Ida. She's here for good, Carrie is here for good, Lila is here for good. Is this the old age I was promised? Tell me that?"

"Carrie and Lila might go home yet," I say. I want to make her feel good.

"Yeah? When the Messiah comes, when it snows on the Fourth of July, when I become an opera singer. You were there. You went with us to see Fay. She's in a loony bin; she belongs in a loony bin. I think I saw something in her face when my Laurence married her. I should have said something then—but hindsight is no sight. Maybe she had a secret?—Everyone has a secret.

"As for the other prize—Rae is here forever. You think Nat is going to come for her? Not when I can support her. As for that Polish *shiksa*—well, what can you expect. Is this her blood? If you remember I never thought Smyrna was a cousin. A crooked deal that was. We brought over a perfect stranger."

Minnie pours tea, sets out a plate of supermarket cupcakes. I lean closer. I think Rae has left the room—yes, probably. Anyway, I lean closer. "You hear from them?" I ask.

"Them?"

"Nat and the Polish girl."

"Never—not a postcard, not a telephone call. All I get sent instead of a birthday present is Raemunde Howard."

"You know why they dumped the kid, Minnie? Is it true—lot of talk in the family—she was on the streets?"

"Lies. They dropped her off at Child Welfare—from their house to Child Welfare."

There is something in Minnie's face. A darkness. But I must be wrong. If there is anything between me and Minnie, it is familiarity. If you were to line up the sisters—why it was Minnie and me, and then Bella and Sophie. My Carl used to say that Minnie doesn't spit but she calls me up to say what color.

And isn't it enough disgrace to be abandoned not once, but twice? Rae robbed Minnie. Yes, robbed her own grandmother. Robbed her of peace of mind. Compared to her other grandchildren, Rae is grief.

Put together all the little girls in the family—what did they want to be? Dancers, nurses, movie stars, teachers. What little girls want to be.

Still, I see Rae on and off for years. Off and on. Half the time when I go to Minnie's, none of you girls are around. But—and this I am sure is the best-kept secret—do you know I am the one who gives Rae her break? I am the one. Probably no one knows. Would she tell?

I remember very well. This is two years later. No, three. My Max is studying for his CPA so that makes it 1966. My friends were sitting in my living room. I was in the split-level on Kenaer Road. That was a house.

These friends—part of an organization, The Wednesday Ladies of North America. Not a sign of them anymore—people move, groups disband. We specialized in cards. Some clubs did mah jong. Our Wednesdays we did cards. That works out perfectly for me because on Wednesdays Carl did poker. We pay state dues, regional dues. Tournaments. Parties. It was nice. But in 1966 a district meeting was to be held in that hall behind Fortunoff's right in Bellport. The works—a banquet, contests, a dance.

What to do? We need a contribution. We are open for suggestions. I get the idea—like a shot. A fortune-teller. *Raemunde the Great.* Dressed up—who would know she is fourteen? My idea gets plenty of negative comment. Yeah, but who has one better?

I call up—I think it was you, Carrie, who answered. Raemunde gets on the telephone. "This is Aunt Ida," I say. "Who?" she says. That's when I decide that instead of a favor—I'll make it a job offer.

"Rae," I say. "My organization—The Wednesday Ladies of North America—would like to hire you."

"You want to hire me?" she says. "What for?"

"It's my idea. I think it would be cute—and not like we are bringing in someone we don't know. For our party at the end of our first convention. To tell fortunes as part of our entertainment. We're also having a singer. Two jugglers. I think a children's chorus—about that I am not certain."

At that point I think I hear her whisper, "I hate telling fortunes."

"Listen," I say, "we'll pay fifteen dollars." This, I made up right on the spot. Now any other girl that age would have said sure or wow or something. Not Rae.

"How many people will be there?"

"Two, three hundred. With husbands—more."

"Then I also want to do a mental act."

"A what?"

"Magic—I have been developing this routine. I'll do it along with fortune-telling. Same price. Oh—I need Lila to assist. She has to get five dollars."

"Not possible," I say. "I have in mind a little booth, curtains. Fortune-telling—you make up something good. That's what I plan. Not on stage—nothing on stage."

"Sure," Rae says. "If you change your mind, give me a call, Aunt Ida. My best to your son Morris."

"Max."

"Max."

First, she tells fortunes. Such a cute booth. I made the curtains myself. A Williamsburg pattern of stripes and tiny roses. You think a setting like that influences her? What an uproar! Where were you, Carrie? You aren't there. Maybe you saw the girls when they dressed? Rae, you couldn't recognize. A gypsy in person. Long skirt, gold loop earrings, a bandanna around her head—shocking. Lila, the same.

But it is the fortunes—the terrible, terrible fortunes. You know what fortune-tellers do—the trips, the tall men, maybe predict a cold, but that's it. She—our misbegotten kin—I didn't know if I could show my face at the next meeting of The Wednesday Ladies.

For the president—for Rose Schnell—Rae predicts a trip down the Amazon to the tip of Colombia where she will be attacked by headhunters. Instead of handsome suitors, she tells three—yes, three—different women that they will be divorced within the next five years. She sees blondes for one husband, a saleswoman for another. She says a purse will be stolen—don't go into the city next Saturday. She tells my Max that he will have to take his CPA exam twice. You think that doesn't put a jinx on him?

Then this powder puff walks out on the stage to do her act. We have her at the end. I'm hoping people might leave first—or talk or eat. On the stage she walks. No glides, slides—who knows when a demon might appear!

"Ladies and gentlemen," she says. "I am Raemunde the Great."

There's a little giggling. I think—thank God. They won't take her seriously. She sprinkles her start-up chat with a Yiddish word here and a Yiddish word there. Now by this time she doesn't look so much like Nat—not that she looks completely unlike Nat. But frankly, she doesn't look Jewish. Not exactly. So from these goyish-style lips—people laugh. And she—she looks pleased.

She sits down on a chair—one wooden chair in the middle of the stage. Holds up her hand for silence. She asks for a volunteer. Like an idiot, Thel's husband, Sy, leaps up; his wife pulls at his sleeve, but too late.

"Sir," says Rae, "here is a white handkerchief. Please examine it for holes. Then kindly fold it and blindfold me."

The fool does.

"Now," says Raemunde the Great, "my assistant will pass among you. Kindly offer her any item you wish for identification."

The assistant is Lila. Rouge, lipstick, a scrawl of mascara—like a second Halloween. She holds up these things.

"That, madam," says Raemunde the Great, "is a silver compact. A present to you from someone dear. An unscratched compact."

That's how it goes. Compacts, handkerchiefs, wallets. And for everything she's got a little story. She tells a man where he left his umbrella. It's uncanny. It's devilish. It's sorcery.

I call Minnie the next day. I tell her everything.

"What did you expect," she says. "It's on your head."

But you, Carrie—eh, I see now. You want real dirt? You're looking for *shlumper* news? All I know is what you read in the newspaper. Three husbands—all right, she's still on number three. What do they call it now? Incompatibility? She could be doing that now—the incompatibility. You should have her followed—this I get from television.

Wait—I see you turn a little red. You *are* having her followed? I bet you didn't get anything—you don't get to be famous by being stupid.

Incompatibility—I could write a book about that. Sex, too. I can tell you—who's alive for it to matter? Every summer we go to the mountains. I hate the mountains—lousy food, biting bugs, four-hour meetings. Yes, meetings. We go to a Workman Circle Camp. Carl loves it and we fight. We fight every stinking August before we go for two weeks. Little Max goes, too. Everybody goes. One year—I don't know how I got the courage—I won't go. No one believes it. I don't go.

I wander around. I never felt that way before—free. I wasn't pretty. I was never pretty—but I had, like, energy. Yes, I had energy. Believe it or not, for two weeks I had a boyfriend. He owned the deli two blocks away. He liked me. "Where's your husband?" he asks. "Away," I say.

You think we talked, made plans. No, it just happens. Every day at three o'clock after his lunch business slowed, he came to me. He had an old uncle on the same floor. How we got away with it, I don't know. Every afternoon he came to me. I put two fans in the window. It was so hot. Feverish-hot. He was a big man, big all over. For two weeks we did it.

You think Rae is the only one in the family with sex? I remember everything—the drops of sweat on my chest, the feeling inside me. Why not? Who will it hurt now? I remember the shape of his body. I remember all this better than my wedding night.

Next year the man sells his deli; he and his wife move away. That wasn't because of me. That was business. What could either of us do? You think it would be different today? You think the times are different? The times are the same. And maybe it wasn't important to him—Mr. Deli Owner. Neither of us ever said that it was important. So he held me in his arms and whispered, *"Schöne mädchen."*

And that's it, Miss Interviewer. I do not understand how Rae turns out the way she does. The famous Miz Magic! I bet she lives in a decent house. Loaded, I guess. If there is any fairness in the world, it wouldn't happen. But there is no fairness in the world.

I remember perfectly well my sister's grandchildren. Lila is a living doll as a kid. Carrie is smart as nails. Rae is nothing.

So it isn't fair.

16

"Leo Littweiler has a *shlong* that reaches his knees. Every morning he says so-long *shlong.*"

"Leo Littweiler has a *shlong* that he wraps around his neck in lieu of a scarf."

"Leo Littweiler cannot for the life of him remember where he left his *shlong*."

We collapse on the bed, springs groan. We laugh and laugh. "Oh God," I say, "the pain of laughter is killing me. My sides are killing me."

"I've got a remedy," says Rae.

"Shut up," Lila says. "The witch will hear us!"

Leo Littweiler picks up Rae soon after the start of her sophomore year in college. Afterward he liked to say they met in the Socialist Club or in Advanced French Literature: Racine and Celine. But actually he went over to her in World History, which was a required course, and started talking. She thinks of him as accosting her, bending over her as she sat. He talks about a movie he saw, how he thought she was in the line way up in front of him. She was there. It is his seeking her out that disturbs her. Because she suspects and despises the reason. She privately calls it weirdo bonding. She is aware that more than not being pretty, she is strange in her manner. She has that spirit of aloneness that marks you. She herself doesn't believe in her impression of plainness—that wasn't vanity, just a sense that no one saw exactly her. In high school she carefully avoided joining the grouping of misfits. She objects to having friends thrust upon her that way.

Leo, on the other hand, rejoices in his ugliness. What I am, he sings, is what I am. What that is—coarse features, log shape, the broad plain of his face shadowed by an ever-present soot of beard. Worse are his chins, those precocious middle-age puddings. Charles Laughton, he says. Don't I look like that poor bastard? he asks. A fleshy gargoyle.

Rae turns away, she ignores.

Still, Leo claims her.

"Where in the name of God," Carrie says, "did Rae find him?"

Lila smiles. "Come on now," she says. "He's not that bad."

"He's horrible," Carrie says. "Obnoxious, pushy, and—he's got hairy hands. He looks like a prototype for a character in *The Great God Brown*."

One evening Leo sits at the table in Washington Heights eating herring salad and explaining his political views. How did he get there? Rae must have invited him.

The next morning Minnie Howard asks Rae outright, "He's not a boyfriend?"

"No," Rae says. "Absolutely not. A friend—period."

"As a friend he is all right."

Show us a trick, Rae, Leo loves to say. Make me disappear.

Isn't it funny how Leo dates a number of reasonably decent-looking girls. He asks Lila for a date. They go for Chinese food and then to a revival of *Desire Under the Elms*.

"I can't believe it," Carrie says.

"Everything with him is, you know, well, amusing. Anyway," Lila says shrewdly, "ugly guys pay you a lot of attention. A lot."

Leo fixes Rae up with a friend. Rae and this boy smoke joints in his car. She speaks about magic, and he nods. He is her first lover. But she can't think of him as that. She alters the thought to first one. That boy is furtive, nervously checking drapes and shades and doors, even though they are never any place where they can be seen.

Unshakable, Leo becomes Rae's steady companion, daily riding the subway with her. What interests Rae is that he is the most observant person she has met—his abilities, she admits, are close to hers. He sniffs her—tells her she uses Pears Soap, scentless shampoo. He reads over her shoulder, notes titles. Why do you like that? he demands. What's that? he says. I didn't hear the answer.

He majors in French literature, he believes in Socialism and also in its impossible impracticality. He prowls the bookstores with Rae. Leo is the one who locates hidden treasures. Spying a copy of Andrews' 1909 edition of *Magic Squares and Cubes* in a bin outside the Strand Book Store. Twenty-five cents. She would have overlooked it, the spine disfigured and cruelly frayed.

They study together in the library, in the evening, then go for coffee. All this time spent in each other's company causes confidences. Afterward, they wonder at the wisdom of these frank confessions to a stranger.

Leo tells Rae how he got drunk at a family gathering, a celebration of *landsleit* for a relative who had safely arrived from Rumania. Then, in a dark corner of a bed buried in coats and sighs of moth balls, he petted heavily with a first cousin named Babs. The evening had culminated hazily with penetration—neither using protection. He had spent a nail-biting two months burdened by textbook horrors of teratology, imagining the reality of a first-cousin, incestuous monstrosity.

Rae tells him the source of her name.

Perhaps it is Leo who starts the rumor that Rae's family were circus people. On the other hand, it is more likely that he is responsible for the Romany story—more his style—in which Rae's gypsy parents, having fallen on hard times, are forced to abandon the life of the transient and sell their daughter.

It is Leo who always sets up little jobs for Rae. "After all," he would say, "you need the money." "Magic," Rae replies, "is composed of tricks—not phony seances." "Hell," Leo says, "fortune-telling is trickery. There isn't that much money to be made in pulling a rabbit out of a hat."

Leo buys Rae her first set of tarot cards and a copy of Mrs. John King Van Rensselaer's book *Prophetical, Educational, and Playing Cards.* He arranges for Rae to tell fortunes at a primary night party of the local Republican club. Rae is paid a flat fee.

Carrie and Lila help Rae dress. The costume, refined through the years, is kept in a suitcase: a long circular paisley skirt, black sweater with a bric-a-brac of gold pins on one shoulder, and a copper-colored silk scarf tied pirate-fashion around her head. "This is stupid," Rae says. "I hate these clothes." "You have to look the part," Carrie says. "It's expected." Rae absolutely refuses the gold loop earrings. Leo comes over with a crystalline globe. "God!" Rae says and bowls it across the room.

This party is held in the Grand Ballroom of a second-rate hotel. They tuck Rae away in a corner behind a curtain of palms. And who can blame them? Rae is not reassuring. Pure hocus-pocus. They have greater hopes for the reflexologist, a husky-voiced, aging blonde.

What happens? Rae watches. First, the standard predictions. Search for clues. If she strikes pay dirt there would be that movement of hand, flap of eyelash, the uncomfortable drawing back. Then the elaboration with each licked lip. Until the person is hooked and, bit by bit, they reveal their own future. That's when Rae gets outrageous—really outrageous. The customers plunge from that leafy corner with flushed cheeks and a sense of adventure. "We're going to win," one man says. "Not a landslide—but a win!"

Does Rae believe in tarot cards? No more than she believes in any dogma of infallibility. It is all illusion. Take the card interpreted as the Juggler. How she moves it can make the client— the victim—gasp. See the Juggler as the One, the Aleph of the Cabala. What shall she tell? That hazard awaits, disease, darkness. It depends on whether the person wants to shiver or be reassured. It is a judgment call.

There is a time when it seems as if Leo really intends to make Rae into a fortune-teller. Not an astrologer. Someone with visions. But she isn't willing, and that might even have magnified his interest. He sets it up for her to tell fortunes at a series of benefits for refugees. Rae says no. How could he, without her permission? Leo tells her she has no social conscience. Children and old men and babies will suffer. Rae puts on a new skirt that foams at her ankles and glows with a confetti of sparkles, and sets

44

forth to tell the future to the superstitious and the eagerly lustful. It is not the kind of magic she knows. Fortunes! Who can tell fortunes? She hates that act. She is never certain which refugees she is saving.

This is where a woman named Sandra—so pleased at the future promised her—mentions Rae to a woman named Gail. Gail wants someone for a children's party. See how it happens? Fortune-telling.

"You know what," Leo says. They are in bed in his cousin Ernie's apartment. They have orders to change the sheets when finished so that someone whose name Rae doesn't hear won't know. This is the first of three times when they make love. Rae is uncomfortable, feels wet. Leo is not fast. He is actually quite slow and exacting. Maybe it's because she does not know what to expect or how to respond that Rae is anxious.

"My mother was fifty-three when I was born," Leo says. "The old man was sixty. Now it isn't that I was a late child—that we were, my sister Rochelle and me. They didn't want kids. Never. But then suddenly they decide—hey, let's have kids for our old age. Like money in the bank."

"I don't believe that," Rae says. She has never met Leo's family.

"True," Leo says. "Absolutely true. My sister—supposedly destined to be the stay-at-home-take-care-of-the-old-folks martyr. What a surprise. Know where she is? Who does? We bailed her out of a jail—in Colorado, I think. Whatever there's to do, our Rochie does it.

"When they die, I'll turn Unitarian. Want some soda? I should have brought liquor. The cupboard is bare."

Leo doesn't show up at graduation. Rae thought he was planning to be there. Otherwise, she certainly wouldn't have gone. Now she stands among the family groups—a gloomy crowd. She joins the periphery of a larger group surrounding a boy she doesn't know. The woman next to her in a brightly colored print dress touches her arm. "He's certainly done splendidly, hasn't he?"

"Yes," Rae says. "He has."

Leo comes over to the apartment to say good-bye. He decided after all to go to graduate school. University of Chicago, he says. He kisses Rae fully on the lips—a hard, acrid kiss. He wishes everyone well. And so long!

Is it possible that Leo has slept with Lila? Why? Lila is glad to see him go. But Lila doesn't say a word.

No one expects to see Leo again. This is one of those suppositions they make. Yet over the years they note that people pass through their lives again and again. It is just the way it is. Sometimes only a glimpse of someone. For instance, that boy—that quiet boy, later named in the newspaper—he has grown up to embezzle millions. The silly girl, plump and unnoticed, later becomes the wife of the politician and stands most sveltely at his side. No one knows. It's all fortune-telling.

G. I. Rosencantz
Sunshine Publishing Co.
Oleana, Fla. 33546–1075

Dear Mr. Rosencantz:

I didn't mail to you Lila's interview because I left a statement she gave me in the restaurant. They had it—but I couldn't get back into the city for a week in order to pick it up. (They wouldn't mail it!) So I sent you what I had in order not to delay payment of expenses.

That's one of the problems of living in the sticks. The city is there, and you are here. Enclosed please find interview and attachment re Dr. Lila Howard. Things are going well with me. Hope your good weather continues.

Fondly,
Carrie Howard

Dr. Lila Howard

My sister. I certainly know her address. Lila has changed. This isn't an absurd observation. I don't mean that she is older. Of course she is older. I mean changed. You would never guess what kind of a child she was if you met her today.

Did I lie to her? "Lila," I say, "I want to talk to you about Rae—formally."

Dr. Howard, my sister and Rae's cousin, is a registered family therapist. She runs her practice from her apartment on the Upper West Side, lots of rooms, went condo five years ago. Lila bought. Look at that, she likes to say, and points out spaces of architectural interest. I guess you might say these days that she is my liaison with Rae.

We agree to meet for the interview at a restaurant that I know Lila likes—Sebastian Seafood.

Lila: This is the weirdest thing I have ever heard. You want to interview me? Your own sister. About Rae. Our childhood, you said—starting at that point. For God's sake, Carrie, you were there. We were there. You are the oldest—Rae really hung around with you in those days, not me. If anyone knows what went on, you do.

Still, no two people have the same garden—even if it is the same garden. But *you* were always there. Except I don't remember you being around so much when Grandma died. Actually, I won't dissemble this way. I know full well where you were on the day of her funeral. You were in bed with Jack, that kid from 6C. In bed in Rae's room—think I didn't know? I wanted to get in—Rae had borrowed my best black scarf for a trick, hadn't returned it. But I can't get in, the door is locked. Rae never locked the door—furthermore, Rae is at that very moment in the living room shouting down Ida and Bella, their words mangled by the gurgle of their fury. So I know it is you. I turn the knob, turn the knob—knowing my grip to be ineffectual. The door will not open. The silence isn't real—a concealing hush, it sounds like people holding their breath. I walk noisily away—clomp-clomp-clomp. Then, I tiptoe back. I hear you. On the day of the funeral.

Anyway, I believe that the funeral of Grandmother Minnie Howard is a seminal point in our lives. Don't interrupt, please! I have given this much thought. She bound us, and when she departs—we unbind. We were a family unit, a simulacrum of a family unit. I believe that the day before Grandmother dies is the last day we are three as one. Last day.

I wrote down my reflections about this last day—good therapeutic release. And I made a copy for you. Here.

INSERT: LILA'S WRITTEN STATEMENT

No one could convince Rae that there isn't magic in religion. And that isn't blasphemy. For instance, the use of significant dreams—the Urim and Thummim. The statements made while in a trance—an authorized trance. "Maybe," Rae says. "But you have to be careful, if you are a wizard or a sorcerer, you are in trouble."

I say that is poppycock. I say she is trying to scare me—we are children at the time. We are kids.

Everyone wants her to tell their fortune. Rae hates that. "How can people be so gullible?" she says. "How could I know what is going to happen?"

The whole thing is a trick. If she knows anything, it is what she has observed. People give themselves away. She is capable of some wonderful howling voices as a medium.

I look this up: The ancient translation of medium means witch.

Carrie is the one who receives the telephone call. She has taken to sleeping during that period on the couch, piling it with blankets and pillows. That is why she hears the telephone. We could have slept until morning—the death had happened; Nurthedge Nursing Home has no sense. Then, too, Carrie could have waited, but she doesn't. She pounds on the doors. She yells, "Wake up! Wake up!"

The message is that Minnie had expired. That's what they said on the telephone. Not died. But expired. She has thrown an embolism. "Thrown," Rae says, "thrown? Sounds funny."

I start crying, and Carrie begins. Rae says that it is all too macabre and we should shut up and she goes into the kitchen to make some tea.

Fortunately, we are not involved in the arrangements. Minnie Howard was a paid-up member of a burial society. It seems that on one of her shopping expeditions, she actually purchased something—a coffin, the plot.

The three granddaughters must be the chief mourners. Everyone says so, despite the boiling grief of Minnie's two living sisters, Ida and Bella.

Some days are better for funerals. Sunshine may be easier on the mourners—but the mood is wrong. Minnie has the right day. A true city-gray sky and a mist of soot that plasters itself on windows. Minnie's sister Bella attends to the details. She offers her house, the contents of her freezer. Doesn't that make sense? The cemetery is in Long Island. Then *everyone* is expected to haul themselves all the way back into the city—when most of them live on the Island side of the Whitestone Bridge. The funeral chapel is directed to deliver the folding chairs to Bella's house. In advance, she would prepare. The chief mourners say all right. We didn't resist.

Carrie and Lila and Rae must order flowers, Bella says. The florist suggests a "Good-bye Arrangement" of white roses, white lilies, white baby's breath, and a generous edging of cheap ferns. The dais on which the coffin rests has flowers front and back.

Everyone at the funeral remarks how well Minnie looks. She is the picture of health in her coffin, with her hair nicely arranged and a small touch of lipstick. Carrie and I go for a last look. Rae stands in the back of the room. Aunt Ida tries to pull her forward. "All your life," she whispers, "you'll regret this."

"Leave her alone," someone hisses.

Ida cries.

This is what Rae remembers Minnie saying to her. She thinks it may have been their last conversation. "There's flesh and blood," Minnie said, "and then there's flesh and blood."

Cousin Aaron gives this eulogy that seems to be about geography as far as anyone could tell. "These are words that carried dreams," he says, "Wielkopolska to Lublin to Cracow to Kielce."

When the casket—a surprising orthodox wood-and-rope box—

slid away, Cousin Aaron leans toward the chief mourners. "Now, girls," he says, "find out who you are. In life, one must find out who you are."

We nod, evade what might have been kisses, and wobble down a path. High heels are a mistake; they dig into the soft sod and leave a trail all the way to the car.

Neither Carrie nor Lila nor Rae are sitting *shiva*—that is the problem. We haven't even suggested that the apartment that Minnie Howard called hers be the site for those that would, or even that we would be "at home." Soft mouths harden at that news; whispers grow dyspeptic.

Families have strange arguments. We have a terrible row, complete with shouts and curses, swiftly and violently exchanged. We are fighting over the disposition of the estate of our shared grandmother, Minnie Howard.

The argument over the inheritance occurs at once. To her beloved sisters, Ida and Bella, Minnie leaves her jewelry. Carrie and I are bequeathed twenty thousand dollars each. Her insurance goes to Cousin Aaron for his many favors. And to Raemunde Howard—she leaves two thousand dollars.

Carrie and Lila say that forty-two thousand split three ways comes to fourteen thousand each and damn the old lady. Rae says no.

How we fight through that long night while strangers consume the glories of Minnie Howard's *shiva* feast. I get a fierce headache, Carrie begins to wheeze, and a map of hives rises on Rae's chest.

Rae, I believe, never regrets any of it—not the results of the quarrel that sends her out into the world with two thousand dollars and desperation.

What is needed, of course, is magic.

I stay in that apartment for two more years. I can't believe it, but I do. Sometimes Carrie is around, sometimes not. The apartment is cavernous, and the cream-colored walls, the long wide hall, the ceiling with patches of flaking paint—all contribute to the empty-nest look. One could imagine rooms filled with Jonathans and Iras and Cynthias spreading their childish cheer, their bicycles and dollhouses. But in truth, this apartment with three bedrooms, a maid's room off the kitchen, and a pantry with a swinging door had never housed anyone before Minnie and Gerald Howard and their son Nathaniel, who had the good sense to go away to college at age sixteen, where the University of Chicago turned him, in his mother's words, into a monster, a worthless political radical who lost all sense of what was proper. Oh yes—and my father, Laurence Howard, the other son. I really can't remember my father.

Everybody is going somewhere. Carrie is joining a movement—I can't remember which. Rae comes and goes with her magic. What are my views? List me as politically apathetic.

It is useless to pretend that I am going to do something dramatic, although for a brief time, when Minnie was in a nursing home, I thought about painting all the rooms in the apartment pure white. But the enormity of the task carried its own disillusion. Instead, I think about improving my mind. I read announcements from the various centers, from Y's and discussion groups. "Spoken Yiddish"; "The Truth about Molochs, Dybbuks, and the Occult"; "Political Theory for the Urban Professional." But what do I want? Do I want the story of *dybbuks?* I want flesh and scent and voice. I am an ordinary young woman, who also happens to be Rae's cousin.

Remember when Rae was on that show in Connecticut? First time on television. Local programming. What was it called? *Kiddie Karnival.* Do you know I saw her? Yes, she invites me to come and see the show. It was—a time of difficulty for me. Yes, I say. That was the beginning of Rae's success.

The children love her. They *really* love her. Mothers watch her sometimes, if they come home early. They perch on the arms of chairs. They giggle. Look at that! The children laugh at different times. They wait. Rae understands that for children part of the anticipation is for the expected. When she pulls out a black-

and-white spotted rabbit instead of the promised white one, she stares at the offending animal, and then shakes her head and says, *"Oy! Oy vay!"* And back comes the refrain from the children in the audience—*"Oy! Oy vay!"*

There is the multicolored scarf—the one that keeps coming and coming. Rae grabs that scarf, tosses back her long hair, and twirls around until the blue velvet cape studded with silver stars rises like a funneling cloud. Max, her assistant, stands at her side. He is a short, gray-haired man, who wears baggy black slacks and a black sweater. Parents enjoy that—such a take-off on the pretty, leggy girl in spangles. Max holds the big spool and slowly winds the scarf around it as Rae pulls more silk from a tiny box. "This better stop," she says. "What will the neighbors think? A *shanda* for the neighbors!"

I am present when that show catches on—not really the show—just her. Only Rae. She calls me up. "Lila, what do you think?"

How do I know what to think?

All across the country—as the show picks up sponsors and affiliates—children go around with new words. Children in Arkansas and Michigan and Utah. A *nosh* of *schnecken,* they beg. They *schlep* their schoolbooks and fear to be a *schlemiel.*

Away from the camera—away from magic—Rae is this awkward, almost graceless woman. She is shy, she stumbles. She drinks a lot of water. That isn't a good sign. When she seems the most amiable—she isn't listening. People meet privately and think about simply replacing her. The world must be full of magicians who could sprinkle in a little Yiddish. Just when they are considering—she brings on the mirror and spinning chair illusion. Puts a kid in the chair and spins him around—in the mirror, the kid looks ten years older. The kids love it.

Am I jealous? Of course, I'm jealous. We are walking down Madison. On a Saturday. We are wearing wool coats, scarves, boots. We had lunch at a sushi bar on Fifty-fourth. I am carrying a newspaper. Rae is carrying a small shopping bag from Lord & Taylor. There is a sameness about us. Suddenly six, eight, ten kids surround us. No—*her*. A harem of admirers. They swamp Rae. Flash autograph books. Sign! Sign! Parents plead to get their kids on her show. So cute, they say.

I control myself. This is what she does, I tell myself. That is her business. Fame intrudes.

I don't know what you expect to learn about Rae. All she does is magic. I know about families, about marriages—that is my business. Whalen left Rae, Rae left Leo, and now she is with Peter. There is nothing unusual in that.

17

The first husband. You would think everyone has first husbands, then second husbands, then third husbands. I, Carrie, have had one husband. One. Not Rae. Not our Rae. Rae has had three husbands. Whalen Clarke is the first husband. And when I say that he could have been mine—he could have been mine. Did Rae take Whalen from me? Steal is more accurate. And I trusted her. Yes, I did.

Think now of Carrie, when in the fall of 1973 she drops out of her classes in fashion design. She is not really less talented than most of the class. But that is the trouble—surely she is meant for more than the churning middle of the crowd. Penuriously, she pecks away at her inheritance from her grandmother.

This is the time when Whalen Clarke picks her up at the museum. Standing side by side in front of a painting. "What?" he says. "Exactly," Carrie replies. They smile. And for two short weeks she is part of his life.

Never has Carrie known a man who owns twenty-seven suits. She stands in this small room, this windowed closet, holding a yellow legal pad and a ballpoint pen. She prints neatly and carefully on the lines, the pen pressing and indenting the pad with the list: 27 suits, 42 shirts, 105 neckties.

Someone carefully constructed that closet with its bleached oak shelves and its waxed rods, all properly spaced, the matching chests of drawers, the plastic boxes on rolling tracks. Like little coffers each plastic capsule holds a shirt folded and stuffed by some arcane service with puffs of tissue. The suits are finely worsted wool varying from chalk-gray to smoke-gray to silver-gray to the gray of cinders and ashes. Unimaginable that the fit is ever faulty or loose. Italian-cut, all those yards of wool. All the shirts bear the same inscription, Made for W. Clarke, in thin black thread embroidered on white. It seems a conceit. Still, perhaps the value is practical. That fine cambric, chambray, oxford cloth—laundered everywhere. The label makes it his. Meant it would come back.

The air is shiveringly cool in that closet. She wears a white cotton nightgown, the lace hem ripped in one flounce where it dangles and makes a loop.

"Planning a robbery?" he says. "Taking inventory?"

She didn't hear him approach. But she waves the pad, not at all embarrassed. After all, he understands her, she thinks. Who she is.

"I'm trying to know all about you."

"Am I my clothes?" He rests one arm on top of a chest, five drawers high. He expects her to say no.

She has to be fair.

"Partially," she says.

This is the first time she sees him naked in the unshadowed light of morning. He stands easily, uncaring, negligently handsome. She knows at once what he reminds her of—a specific photograph in a textbook, in a chapter entitled "Classical Antiquity." A kouros. A sculpted naked man at whose image she had stared so long that another student named Denise Parker told her that her interests were surely prurient. But it is the perfection of the form that surprised her. She decided that it was unreal, totally idealized, from the Herculean shoulders to the crown of loose curls, even the abundance of pubic hair pulled from marble strand by strand. Later she sees similar statues in a museum.

She stares at Whalen so steadily that she suspects her face will redden, and that will make him laugh. She turns around to conceal the girlish warmth. Touches a drawer.

"How many sweaters?"

"I have no idea," he says and reaches out to grasp her shoulders firmly and turn her back.

Whalen, at age twenty-nine, works for a multinational corporation with a name that changes from country to country and has a passport stamped with the permissions of half the countries in the world.

He and Carrie sleep together in a bed shaped like a sleigh that once belonged to his parents.

The next time Rae sees Carrie is at breakfast. She has come back to spend the weekend in the apartment—Minnie Howard's old apartment—where Lila and Carrie still live.

"Well," says Rae, "I see that you have met a man, are sleeping with him, having a good time, and thinking about the wild blue yonder."

"How did you know?" Carrie puts down the half of a bagel on which she is spreading cream cheese. "I mean really—how did you know? You just walked in and I haven't said a word. Not one word. You do have a power, Rae, you know that—a power."

"My God!" Rae says.

G. I. Rosencantz
Sunshine Publishing Co.
Oleana, Fla. 33546–1075

Dear G. I.:

Enclosed please find some notes. I am aware that nothing here is—shall we say—properly salacious, or even secret. But I believe that I am getting there. "Working" the material in a matter of speaking.

Anyway, the enclosed notes cover the early meeting with Whalen Clarke. I call this to your attention so that you won't decide at this point that I am the "woman spurned." Did I *know* Whalen first? You bet your booties that I did. And yes, I was crazy about him. If you were a woman, you would understand. Imagine walking into—no, simply walking anywhere—and having other women stare. The reason? You are with this supreme man—this total Number 10 on any scale.

Yes, I warned Rae. How can you expect to hold him? I said. He's a WASP demi-god. You amuse him for a moment. The exotica of the *other*. You, Rae, I said, are the other. And even if we forget the obvious. Let's turn to sociology, I said. He's upper class—education, culture—forget money. And we, Rae, are not. The best you can say about us is working class—maybe a half step above. If you think this doesn't really matter in America, think again. You'll never keep him, Rae. Absolutely never.

I am trying to reach Leo Littweiler—Rae's second husband. I can't get past his secretary in L.A. Have you any suggestions? What do your people usually do?

Yours,
Carrie

18

Rae was always an indifferent student in college. Weekends, she works parties as the hired magician. Cards are printed— *Raemunde the Great.* She prefers children's parties. She likes the way they respond to magic. They cannot be fooled. They inspire her.

She begins to be noticed. Good with children, someone says. Guaranteed to keep them quiet. Suddenly Rae keeps a notebook listing dates and places. One month she has six parties.

She lives by referrals. One takes her to a large house on Long Island. In Great Neck. Twenty children, ages four to five. They cluster around her, party children in the uniform of brightly colored corduroy pants and striped shirts. No frilly dresses, no petticoats, no tiny suits. Party time for the rich.

There on that soggy, shamrock-green lawn she will meet Whalen Clarke. In the spring sunshine. Who is the birthday girl? Here comes the birthday girl in shocking-pink overalls. She is Whalen's niece.

Does Rae's heart go pitty-pat? Who knows. Don't think that Carrie and Lila and Rae didn't think about that ultimate carrot—Mr. Right. You can scoff—but everyone wants it.

Rae doesn't know about Whalen at that moment. She no longer lives in Minnie Howard's apartment. So she never saw Whalen bring Carrie home and kiss her sweetly on the lips—right outside the door that led to Minnie Howard's apartment.

Where did Carrie meet him? Whalen picked her up at the Museum of Modern Art. It was a Picasso exhibit. She said that he spoke first.

And this is how life works when you are good—word of mouth. Whalen mentions to Carrie that his sister wants an entertainer for the party. That's how it happens. It is always simple. Carrie suggests Rae. Perhaps she writes the name and telephone number on a scrap of paper torn from an envelope and Whalen gives that paper to his sister. But Carrie never introduces Rae to Whalen. That part isn't so.

Rae's approach to very young children is to present herself as an amateur, as if they are all in this together. To give them a stake in whether or not the tricks work.

Her show takes place on the back lawn—an area with a large tree for hiding behind. The children behave as she commands, obeying with communal awe. At the end of her performance, Rae bows, and the children, coached by mothers, applaud.

She sees the man watching her. A good-looking man, and so she smiles. Wouldn't anyone? Whalen comes over and introduces himself. He brings Raemunde the Great a cup of punch. His sister watches, she talks to people, but she still watches.

Perhaps they laugh, perhaps Rae looks too much at ease. She is a nice woman, his sister. She has been polite and pleasant. Her name is Hildegarde and she wears a homespun gray skirt and a matching vest.

"That was a good show," Hildegarde says, standing between Rae and Whalen. "The children enjoyed it. Here's your check for your fee."

Her feelings are obvious, complete with the dismissal smile.

There are times when people should meet you. Times when your life can be changed. Therefore, Whalen met Rae at the right moment. A period of eccentricity in the style of the world. It made her seem—albeit briefly—all right. The wildness of her hair, the appearance of having assembled herself rather quickly, the intensity. Yes, even her clothing fits. Historically, Rae thinks of this as the exact point in life at which she looked the most desirable.

"What do you mean?" Carrie says. "Whalen Clarke asked you out?"

"You haven't seen him for four months—you said that," Rae says. "Isn't that what you said? God, we have always done this. I mean unless it is someone special. Lila and you and me. We have always traded."

"I'm not trading!"

19

You can't live on parties. Rae finds a job in the office of an insurance company—never a full week, which suits her. She still has two thousand dollars in the bank. She frequents magic shops. Even meets a few of the old masters. And living alone, she has time to perfect certain tricks of her own. She begins development of the early version of the spinning mirror, a variation on Indian levitation without hydraulics, and also a new twist on P. T. Selbit's woman sawed in half.

Sometimes, Rae won't answer the telephone. When I'm working, she says to everyone with annoyance. Call back tomorrow. And stop, Carrie, with those phony emergency telegrams—begging me to pick up the receiver. You don't understand absorption.

Carrie doesn't understand absorption? Maybe not. But Carrie understands Whalen Clarke. Magic could not have invented Whalen Clarke. He is a man who makes women turn around, swivel their heads like the lovelorn eyeing a body.

Carrie says this right away to Rae, because the incongruity of Rae and Whalen being together requires emphasis. After all, Rae is a half-orphaned child whose father lives in an unknown place, and whose personal past is certainly a murky hole.

Once Whalen picks Rae up at the office and is seen. Afterward her friend Dottie says that Whalen is too perfect. And this was not said unkindly. Whalen is the statue come alive, the King of the Prom. Such a terrific, cultured, and ever-polite man.

What does Rae usually prefer? Men with dark hair; men whose heritage she understands. Whose physical cues are sure and quick. Then they might or might not see you again. Doesn't matter.

Whalen is a family name, the maiden name of his great-grandmother. Her father had been a physician in Baltimore. Whalen took Carrie to the Metropolitan to see his ancestor's picture: a nineteenth-century large canvas of a group of men in morning coats and hats grouped around a hapless patient on a cot, a pale woman, her hair artfully arranged. That's him, Whalen said and pointed out a face, third from the left, second row. A stout man, with a sharply pointed beard and a self-assured expression on his face. Carrie noticed that all the men in the painting face the viewer rather than the patient—probably long dead.

Carrie believes that Whalen Clarke was once hers. Furthermore, she didn't lose him; rather, the relationship was dug out from under her. She fell, she used to say, into a trap of deceit.

She was pursuing a career. What career? Never mind. She was seeing Whalen Clarke—and she had trusted those close to her. He could have been hers, life could have been different. The landscape of her future could have been different.

This is absurd, Rae says. A battle, a fierce, screaming battle takes place in the living room of Minnie Howard's apartment.

Listen, the market for magicians is relatively narrow. She could type. Her supervisor calls her "Good old Rae." She is vulnerable, yearning—her friend Leo vanished after graduation. Good luck, kiddo, he said. Quite suddenly, she is alone.

This is what she confesses to Lila and Carrie.

20

Yes, she got him. When I want to be mean, I say she used a spell. Now, I don't believe that exactly. Still, literature is full of love potions, their efficacy and dosage. Something could have spilled from a beaker. Rae the Magician!

When Rae plans her marriage to Whalen Clarke, she has to make a list of guests—from her side. She doesn't want to do that—she doesn't have that kind of family. So it is annoying. She sits in her kitchen and chews on the eraser end of a yellow No. 2 pencil.

Who? Who to ask? She is twenty-two years old. The family is basically dead or lost. At least the part of it she knows. Her friends decimated by differences and time.

The wedding has gotten out of hand. What Rae wants is a manageable event, with a discernible beginning and end. She envisions a room for the ceremony—judges have offices. She would wear a dress—new dress, blue silk. Then she and Whalen would go back uptown for dinner. Pick a restaurant—one with those balloon shirred shades on the window, a name in scrolled gold paint. Who at the table? Twenty people. Twenty is a good number. Whalen knows twenty people. She would ask Carrie and Lila and maybe Dottie from work.

Whalen says that his sister Hildegarde wants to host the wedding at her home in Great Neck. A wedding gift from her. A way of making up for the fact that she doesn't welcome Rae. Whalen kisses Rae's neck, his fingers caress the skin beneath her sweater. It is for his sister. They are so close.

Celebrations, if not tied down, can free float, can be claimed. The wedding now belongs to Hildegarde. Such a beautiful tent on her lawn where the grass slopes to the tiny artificial pond. All of this is why Rae has to make a list. But who should be on it? Carrie and Lila. Minnie Howard's sisters bond together and send a beautiful appliquéd bedspread.

Two ancient widowed cousins who live together in Park Slope respond. They are delighted to attend. It will be an outing. Rae invites Mr. and Mrs. Abe Harter. She once worked for the man at Harter Lumber Company. They will come, although Rae knows that Mrs. Harter thinks that Rae has gotten too big for her britches. Bit by bit, Rae assembles a list of names to receive the cream-colored, heavily engraved invitations. She doesn't really care if anyone shows up—but she has to have names for Hildegarde. It is then that Rae decides to invite Leo Littweiler and guest even though she has not seen him or heard from him in years. She uses his parents' address.

Rae wears Hildegarde's wedding dress. Hildegarde is amazed that it fits her, that it has to be taken in at the bust and waist. You look stunning, Hildegarde says. In acres of white peau de soie and a headdress made from points de France lace from the province of Beaujeu. Hildegarde's great-grandfather brought that lace as a gift for his bride-to-be when he returned from his grand tour in 1855. The lace is incurably yellowed.

Will Carrie come? Of course. She wouldn't give them the satisfaction. She is escorted by a tall elegant man with deeply gray hair whom she met at Balducci's.

Leo rushes across the lawn when he sees Rae; half running by his side, to keep up, is a petite brunette, a good four inches shorter than he. Leo crushes Rae's borrowed dress in his hug. *"Mazel tov,"* he says, then he pulls back and pushes forth the tiny brunette. "Meet Penny—my wife."

Penny smiles sweetly. "Gorgeous wedding," she says. "What a setting."

Do they say any more? Rae thinks not. Others appear. Whalen curves his arm protectively around her shoulder. "Mrs. Margaret Linwood," he says and introduces Rae. "Mr. Xavier Winston, Carla Tetheran."

Three, four times as Rae looks around, she sees Leo. He waves, he winks. Once she makes out what he silently mouths in her direction. "How's the magic business?" She half fears, testing a nightmare, that he will suddenly clap with those powerful hands of his and silence the guests. Now, he will say, for the finale, a few minutes of prestidigitation from herself—the bride.

When Rae is in a bedroom and taking off the wedding dress, sliding the wrinkled garment back on its extra-wide padded hanger, and putting on her gray suit, she realizes that Leo did not invite her to his wedding to Penny.

21

Carrie and Lila and Rae. I go one way, Lila another, and Rae, a third. That's what happens. To tell the truth, most of this separating is Rae's fault. She sees me when she has to—and barely. It annoys the hell out of me when people say—Weren't you once so close? What does that mean *so close?* We were close as kids. Kids are one thing, adults another. Friends, I always say, change.

But whatever made these changes was Rae's fault. Her responsibility. I can't help feeling that—somewhere, somehow—Rae snatched my future. How did it happen?

Sometimes Carrie thinks about when they were together. Carrie and Rae. The mischief they plotted—two orphanlike girls. And they took the blame for each other. It was for Rae's sake that

Carrie brazenly stood up and said, I did it. They were threatened—promised a dark future. And when Rae wasn't asked to that special dance, didn't Carrie arrange for her to have a booth to tell fortunes?

Rae's fortunes were the shock of the evening. Carrie and Rae had set Lila to work for days gathering gossip. And she had. What Rae told!—afterward the girls were nearly expelled.

Carrie always believes there is enough time.

And there is hardly ever enough. So time makes Carrie into the wife of Dunstead, who works in the office of a factory that makes strangely shaped screws. Carrie spends long hours decorating her house. She has huge buckets of glue and savagely slaps wallpaper on the walls. She does the work herself—the painting, the shelves. It costs next to nothing, she tells her husband and hides the bills. She's trying for a background of elegance. But that's hard.

They own a split-level house in upper Rockland County. The house has a brown roof. The very house that Carrie decorates again and again. Dunstead celebrates each change by climbing on top of Carrie and creating in her what he takes to be a shiver of joy.

Carrie's sons are named Robert and Scott. They are close in age to the sons of Rae's third husband, Peter. Carrie says that Rae cares more for Peter's sons by another marriage than she does for her own nephews.

When Rae sends tickets to her show for Robert and Scott, they are conspicuously absent. Two empty seats in the first row. Two other fortunate children are quickly escorted down the aisle. The seats filled.

22

Through Whalen's connections, Rae begins a career as a banking trainee. It is absurd. Rae calls Lila on the telephone. "I am not fit for that job," she says. "What am I going to do? I try, I smile, I bought two suits with appropriate colored pocket handkerchiefs. I did all this for Whalen."

Lila wants to say, You made your bed. On the other hand, she doesn't want to close off all communications.

Whalen is always sensitive to the moods of life. He's the one who insists that they find a new apartment. That everything between them be new. Look, Rae says, I won't pretend—He is a bridegroom of splendor.

They move to an apartment on Sixty-fourth Street off Lexington. She is scared—she has never spent so much money in her life. The decorator says something, and Whalen says all right.

In that apartment, they entertain friends. Rae contributes Dottie Madison and her lover, Philip. The others are Greg Harper, the Lymans, the Spauldings, and occasionally Dominic Rutkin. They eat together; they play together in the country. The wives mostly have careers. Rae is in banking.

Whalen travels. He is gone two weeks out of every month. Rae is always thinking about magic. But she waits until Whalen is away. It takes courage for her to put up her first notice. After all, she is no longer in circulation. Magician, it says, Parties for Children. The money is unimportant. She could specialize. Children only.

The notice is tacked to the bulletin board in the Food Emporium. Then Rae places a discreet sign in the corner of the window of Children's Feet. She slips the salesman twenty dollars.

Perhaps marriage or contentment is responsible—Rae is a success. Who could believe it? She could do parties twenty, thirty days a month. At first, she thinks she should turn down some. Oh, but she can't.

Her work at the bank suffers, the result of disorganization. The manager calls Rae into an inner office. The man is not unsympathetic. He knows Whalen. "Tired," he tells her. "You look tired. But nevertheless," he says, "you must learn to give yourself where it is important." He pats her on the shoulder. "I'll consider that," Rae replies.

In spring, Whalen and Rae go to Bermuda for two weeks. She sends postcards to Carrie and Lila. Whalen disappears for three of those days, so perhaps it is partly a business trip. After they return, Rae takes over the maid's room; they don't have live-in help. In that room she begins sustained work on the development of new tricks, the acquisition of others into her repertoire. She learns more about what children want—the dazzle, the surprise, the laugh.

Rae calls Lila. "I have to tell him," she says.

"Be careful," Lila advises. "Consider the consequences. It's on your head, you know."

Rae sets it up. All the obvious devices. The candlelight dinner, the seductive manner. She doesn't want to hurt him.

"Whalen," she says, "I want to leave my job—I am wasted there."

"I don't understand," Whalen says. "Rae, if you want to leave—leave."

"I thought it might not be good—you arranged the job."

"A job," he says and kisses her. "Not an indenturing."

"I'm sorry. But I am mad for magic."

"I know."

23

It happened as I knew it would happen—and I never pretended to be sorry. That would have been totally hypocritical. There was going to come a day when Whalen was not going to be interested. He is a man of substance. And his wife—our Rae—is like a servant, a hired performer. Magician at kiddie parties. At some point, she would crush his sensitivity. The end was inevitable. There is a limit to how many rabbits she could pull out of a hat.

Rae calls Lila.

"I'm going to California," she says, "Los Angeles."

"Vacation? How long?"

"Lila, I'm moving to L.A."

"You're kidding? Did Whalen get transferred? When are you leaving? What about the apartment?"

"God," Rae says, "don't you hear the nuances? I thought you specialized in that. *Me,* Lila, I'm leaving. Only me."

"So that's it—the split. Listen, Rae, don't run away. That's my advice. My advice to everyone. And after your grieving period— I know a man who would be perfect for you. But first, do counseling. I know someone on Forty-seventh Street."

"What?"

"Therapy—you and Whalen should immediately go into counseling. It will be a revelation. And this person—my friend—she is absolutely the right one. She's fair, but tough. She'll take no shit from you."

"We aren't going into counseling, Lila. I'm going to L.A. On Wednesday. Whalen is staying here. I think he's staying here."

"You aren't listening, Rae. You should permit the emotional dust to settle. That is what I always advise. It's sex, isn't it, Rae?"

"Yes."

"Men can be bastards, Rae. But Carrie warned you—not that I ever excused her behavior. Nevertheless, she warned you."

"I'll write or call from California. Send my address."

"What about the apartment? All that beautiful furniture?"

"Whalen has it—he has everything."

"Oh, God—you need a lawyer. I bet you don't have one. Rae? Rae?"

G. I. Rosencantz
Sunshine Publishing Co.
Oleana, Fla. 33546–1075

Dear G. I.:

I loved your last issue—particularly "The Tramp on the Steamer." You truly put your finger on the dangers of cruise groupies. It was "steamy" *(sic).*

But to get down to details. I took your advice. Didn't try to get past Leo Littweiler's secretary—I offered her the coin of the realm instead. Unfortunately, she wouldn't give me a receipt—so you will have to take my word for it that I gave her two hundred dollars ($200). Believe me, in the long run, it will be worth it. Evelyn (the secretary) was willing to talk. I felt that this should be a face-to-face meeting (see attached). Again, I'm afraid, a lunch was required (see attached). But Evelyn has been with Leo for years and is the veritable fount of information. She was a guest at the wedding and the divorce.

Expenses re meeting with Leo Littweiler's secretary:

Bribe to secretary	200.
Air fare (nonrefundable ticket)	348.
NYC to LA (Stayed with friend—so no hotel, meals, etc.)	
Lunch at "Gaudy Salad"	64.

Fondly,
Carrie Howard

24

This is my theory. I call it the Twelve Blocks of Life Theory. I believe that everyone's life has twelve geographical and psychological blocks. Certain people belong within these parameters. They walk in and out all the time.

Rae doesn't know that Leo Littweiler is in Los Angeles. Even if she knew, she wouldn't call him. She is more concerned with recent events. Her thoughts diverted. The reason is the divorce. The loss of Whalen Clarke. She can hardly believe her magic was a success in Connecticut—you are on top, you vanish, you are forgotten.

Being a form router at Fritsch & Potter is a nothing job. It leads nowhere and no one stays. Usually there are an even dozen routers, mostly women. The routers receive the forms first, separate them, fill out the transmittal slip, and paper clip it. Rae calculates that the median age of routers is 23.4. She is then old at twenty-five.

They are attractive—the routers. Two years ago a woman named Louise married a man who worked on the floor above and entered another life. But generally the job is a stopgap—the routers plan to be actors or singers or dancers. That is their real life.

Rae works mornings until noon. That leaves afternoons free for those days when she has a children's party to do. Connections are hard to make in L.A. She knows no one there. She puts up signs on supermarket bulletin boards offering her services. A woman calls her.

"Could I by chance," the woman said, "have seen you on TV back East on a kiddie show in Connecticut?"

"Yes," Rae said.

"I thought so—from the name. You were a scream. A real scream. Are you available?"

"Yes."

"I'll tell my husband."

Her future traveled on this slight chance. Because of Connecticut, Rae gets to do a three-minute act on a show—a clown show. The clown isn't happy. That has nothing to do with Rae. My life, he tells her, is fucked up. Plenty fucked up. I like you, Rae. You're sweet. But remember, he says, kids are fickle.

Rae becomes a regular. She needs a new name. The clown's name is Ralph. No Raemunde, he says. Rae nods. Call me Miz Magic, she says. But she doesn't quit her job as a form router right away. The show could vanish.

For a time, it is cute, it is amusing. People from the office call each other. Did you see Rae on television? they ask. She's a scream.

Like a kiddie's Fanny Brice. Try to catch her—she's on through the summer.

These are the people Rae knows the longest. The people from Fritsch & Potter. She registers for a class at USC. Sometimes, she goes to a bar called Leon's.

It is put to her very frankly. The show has gone to your head, Rae is told. Success has gone to your head. This is said first by a woman named Laura. She and Rae sit side by side in the evening class of Speak in French at USC. After class they go to Leon's together.

Other people say that Rae is lucky. Save your money, advises the chief accountant at Fritsch & Potter. Remember, he adds, I knew you when. Anyway, fads come and go—think of the Hula-Hoop, think of Tiny Tim. Save your money.

Later Rae acquires new friends. Friends who only know her as Miz Magic. At a party someone asks her if she didn't used to go by the name Raemunde the Great. Yes, she had. Well, when he visited his family—they lived in Bellport—his brother said that she had done a children's party at his house. My brother, the man said, thought that you were a gypsy. He said he had asked you, and you said that Raemunde was your real name.

25

Leo Littweiler says that he was the first person to call Rae Miz Magic. "I never thought that fortune-telling was for her," he said. "She isn't a gypsy after all. No, I thought some kind of a classy clairvoyant act. Something challenging. There is a lot of money to be made in that. And to tell the truth, Rae has a certain knack. But she chose the safe way. Entertaining kids."

Still, in many ways, he believes he is responsible for the general outline of her act. He considers her a brilliant creation. Where she interceded is in presenting herself solely for children.

26

Rae is never certain exactly what Leo does. He is in the business. He is a friend of Harold Powell's. And as the saying goes—Any friend of Harold Powell . . . Harold Powell is responsible for much of Rae's success. She has never actually met him. But she is regularly invited to his parties. What he once said about her has been quoted: "I appreciate that woman."

One Sunday, she is standing by the pool. She wears blue jeans and a sleeveless T-shirt. Her stance is a slouch. The sun makes her squint, and she looks down. So Leo reaches her side before she sees him. He looks the same—almost. He's filled out, appears harder, seems tighter.

"It's you," Leo says. "My God, it's Rae."

"Leo? Leo?" She stares as if she can't quite place him.

"I didn't know you were out here," he says. "You look great, Rae. What are you doing these days?"

"I do a show on television. For kids."

"Hey—magic. That's right—I heard. Miz Magic. Miz Magic strikes again. Your husband come out here with you?"

"Divorced. And how is your family?"

"See over there—the blonde in the black slacks. That's my wife, Linda. We have kids, we have two kids. Can you imagine me, Rae, with children named Claude and Erica? Beats all, doesn't it?"

"She's gorgeous."

"Linda. Yeah, she is a princess. Stop staring, Rae. I lucked out, that's all. My golden girl."

Rae telephones Lila in New York City:

"Lila, you will never in fifty million years guess who I saw this afternoon!"

"Who?"

"Leo. Leo Littweiler."

"In L.A.?"

"Absolutely. And he is married—again. Not that girl we met at my wedding. Lila, the new one is a blonde and at least six inches taller than Leo. She's a total blonde. She's a knockout. And he's got two kids."

"Imagine—imagine that. Our dumpy Leo. What's he do?"

"I don't know. Something important, I think. It's astonishing. When I met her—the wife, Linda—well, I thought she might be a face. You know—only a face. But she is more. That's the surprise."

"Then he's rich, Rae. If she looks like that and has a mind and Leo looks like he does, he's rich."

27

The Twelve Blocks of Life—Rae, for instance, met her third husband before she married her second. I don't know Peter well—but well enough. I would have said that he is not Rae's type. The man is moody. He is picky—goes at you like a gnat. Peter Anson. But she met him in California before she married her second husband. I suppose when he went away, Rae thought that was the end. But it wasn't. That's why the theory works.

The year Peter has his Guggenheim, he has an invitation to go to California. Nothing is what he expects. First, his girlfriend, Patty, changes her mind about going with him and stays in New York. Afterward, Peter says that you must meet people at the right time. He admits that sounds mystical. Nevertheless, if you meet people at the wrong time nothing takes. Sometimes that ends it, sometimes not.

When Peter picks up Rae at the USC library, he really doesn't know who she is—only that she looks New York. And he is homesick.

"You looked smug," Peter says. "Really smug, Rae." She is in the kitchen, facing the sink and the window. It is too dark to see a view, the Hudson River. But it is there, a ribbon of water going straight to the city.

He hasn't told her she is on the news, because by the time she left the kitchen her image would have vanished from the television screen. He leans against the doorframe holding his drink—something crystal clear.

"Did I?" she says.

"Like the cat who swallowed you-know-what," he says.

She is making an early supper. Four people are coming over. She is making her special grilled radicchio and *rigatoni, salsiccie, e funghi.* She made the salad in the morning because Peter likes his salad greens very dry.

When the telephone rings, it is Vera, her agent. "You were on the news," she says. "I was right about the light blue dress—that worked out perfectly."

"Yes," Rae says. "You were right."

She has a pitcher of Bloody Marys all ready and a pile of finely chiseled celery sticks. Shifton arrives first. "Well, here she is," he says. "The star."

Lettey Patrick brings red wine. She always calls in advance; her mother taught her that. She asks what is wanted—so she brings three bottles of Gamay Beaujolais. "We saw you," she says. "Dick said to me look, look. I was dressing. What was the award for? Anyway, congratulations. Dick is parking. He was funny. When that man presenting droned on, blah, blah, blah, that's when Dick said it was a slow day—no plane crashes, no couple trussed and bound and slaughtered in a locked room, no excavated mummified remains from the second century. Just Rae."

Everyone says the pasta is a success. "You are a splendid cook," Shifton says. "Yum." The woman named Elaine who had been invited for Shifton smiles at him. She brought a rhum baba, not requested. Rae has a bowl of quivering orange Bavarian cream waiting. She serves both. She slices the rhum baba into thick syrupy slices and piles them on a platter.

"What's next for you, Rae?" Lettey asks. "And by the way, my cousin's daughter says that you are really something—she's four."

"Did you know that when Rae was a child and told people that she was going to be a magician when she grew up, they said that she would outgrow it?" Peter says. "She told me that." He looks at Rae. "You did tell me that? Compare that, for instance, with if she had said she wanted to become a teacher or a nurse—no one would have said you'll outgrow it. Right?"

"I'm going on tour," Rae says.

"What?" Peter looks up, a frown pleats his forehead and vanishes.

"Yes," Rae says. "They want to do the show from a few different cities."

"Is that wise?" Shifton says. "Something like what you do is relatively fragile, I would imagine."

Rae gets up to clear the table.

Peter says that he is working. He has momentarily given up his scholarly activities to accept a bitsy role. He is playing an idiot younger son in *Summer Gladiator*.

"Hey," Peter says when Rae comes back with the tray of coffee cups. "I meant to ask—who was that ugly man I saw you with yesterday? Talk about the apeman cometh."

28

What started me thinking about Rae? It was the personal notice—the one in the AFL-CIO newsletter asking about her father. No one I know saw it. The long, long vanished Nathaniel Howard. My uncle. Also, according to Lila, Rae is apparently planning to take what she calls a sabbatical. This I heard about first from Lila. Later, it was in the newspaper. That's why I knew the time was ripe for the truth about Raemunde Howard. Miz Magic. Now she's put an ad in the *Times*.

Vera is well established as a theatrical agent when Leo Littweiler introduces her to Rae. So much has happened in Vera's life since then that she mistakenly thinks that her relationship with Rae goes back forever.

She is always mentioning events to Rae. As if Rae were present at Ric Chatham's famous party or came to the Sunday brunches that she and Sidney used to have in that wonderfully ancient house on the coast fifteen miles south of L.A. Vera will say that Sidney was the love of her life. If she is in the mood, she says that Sidney will always be the love of her life. He died one Saturday morning in 1976 on the way to Santa Barbara. His car collided with an old Dodge Dart driven by a fat man wearing a blue undershirt. Sidney died instantly. So did the teenage girl in the other car, her rayon slip twisted up around her shoulders. Where was Sidney going at such a reckless pace at eight in the morning on a Saturday? Vera varies the errand.

Rae is Vera's star client. Sometimes Vera stares fiercely at her. She does not remember whether, in the blurry, tear-ridden days after Sidney's death, she confessed that he was planning to leave her—although not that day. That he had hooked himself up with a stoned bitch who was really famous.

What is true is that when Rae meets Vera in L.A., Sidney is already dead two years, and Vera's daughter, Josephine, is three years old and sweet and lovable. It would be ten years before Josephine, enrolled in family therapy, would sit in Lila's office, her lips twisted as she screams hysterically about the urgencies of her hate.

In analysis, Vera speculates about what makes Rae succeed. I search, she says, for the *mot juste*. It is true that Rae is obsessive about what she does—talk about confidence! But she possesses none of the benchmarks of success. Where are the charm and the looks—basically, and here Vera laughs wisely, Rae is just a bag of tricks.

Vera sits behind her desk, a glowing expanse of African mahogany. She wears a low-cut white silk blouse—she has that same style in fifteen different colors. Her breasts are small and high, and her skin is childlike in its untouched smoothness. Even when male friends don't care to pursue a relationship, they appreciate this resplendent view.

Vera's office is opulent, a model of reflective glass. It does not look like a working office, but Vera works very hard.

"What can I get you?" Vera asks.

"Coffee," Rae says. "I had this terrible lunch."

Vera nods. Secretaries like being employed in Vera's office, so they don't mind bringing coffee.

"I think," Vera says, "that a lot could be nipped by coming out with a story about this leave you plan to take, the sabbatical, like you were going off to perfect new tricks or something. It's the void that causes problems. Because that allows speculation—and nothing is worse.

"I heard AIDS yesterday, or you were checking into Betty Ford, and then that you were joining a cult. Even planning to learn the secrets of black magic. That's why I tie this all in with this guy who's calling people about you. And his questions—know what he asked me? He wanted to know why you stopped telling fortunes, how you felt about for-God's-sake your grandmother, did you ever hear from your real father—and we'll talk about that, kiddo—did you ever consider divorcing your present husband, why did you divorce Leo Littweiler, and on and on.

"As a person who performs for children—there are limits. Divorce is all right. But even there—it has to be incompatibility, not scandal. So we have to think, we have to consider.

"Rae, this telephone voice has got dates and names. You think he has your diary? You don't keep a diary, do you? And why did you put that stupid advertisement in the *Times?* You really want to find this father? My father didn't walk out on me—and I certainly don't want to find him, anyway. Rae, everyone is very unhappy with you."

G. I. Rosencantz
Sunshine Publishing Co.
Oleana, Fla. 33546 – 1075

Dear G. I.:

I digress for a purpose. Let me say that I loathe Rae's agent. I met her once—no, twice. Anyway, what I hear is that she is getting questions about Rae after that ad in the *Times*. The person asking these questions is *not* me. What I want to know—I'll

mince no words—is it you? In short, are you fucking me? Have
you assigned someone else Miz Magic's story? Rae is mine. My
idea. My cousin.

Yours truly,
Carolyn Howard

Carolyn Howard
Box 117
Crosby Falls, N.Y. 11172

Dear Ms. Howard:

   Don't be paranoid. I have no idea who is asking questions
about Miz Magic. Maybe it is a fan—they do these things. Anyway, I am still waiting for your "exposé" of this woman. Are you
concealing anything? And is what you are concealing the reason
that someone else is asking questions—to beat you to the punch?

Yours truly,
G. I. Rosencantz.

29

First Rae doesn't see or hear from Leo for years. Then they become
pals. Rae sends Lila a clipping about Leo Littweiler's divorce, from the
Los Angeles Times. And a note that Lila shows to me: "I'll tell you something, Lila. But promise not to mention this. I swear that I knew that
Leo and his Linda would be divorced. I saw a paper—a shimmering
paper—like a *get*. Remember when Aunt Fannie divorced Jerry? She
had this paper from the rabbinical court. She used to wave it around.
My *get*, she would say. Legal divorce."
   Lila writes back: "The man is a *putz*. When you told me that the wife
was good-looking, I knew divorce was inevitable."

30

No one understands when Rae starts seeing Leo. It's clear that she has had an argument with the man from New York. He moves back to his own apartment. But Leo as an option?

When does it start? It starts at Rio's. Rio's is a restaurant with a decor of graffiti. Theory was that the owner had pulled in three, four boys, given each one hundred dollars, spray cans of paint, brushes—go to it. The walls have everything—from words seen everywhere to vulgar outlines showing variants of copulation. Also, there is the affectation of bare-bulb lighting. Rio's was a place of confrontations fueled by that atmosphere—arguments, snide remarks, partners exchanged.

Rae is in Rio's with Leo and his new friend Molly. Molly is blonde. Ignore the name. Blonde, parchment-thin, tanned. She is talking about a wonderful doctor. A miracle man.

Leo laughs. Miracle men! He went to such an individual once. A plastic surgeon—highly recommended, expensive as sin. Yes, the doctor said. He could remake that face. He made a sketch and showed Leo a computer-enhancement. Startling, Leo said. Like someone else. He couldn't stand the thought. So he went home and later paid the physician's consultation fee. More than Leo once spent in a month. But that was long ago.

A man comes up to them. He could have thought that Leo was there with Rae, and Molly was up for the taking. Why not? Two dark-complected Jews, and Molly—the golden captive princess, smiling with pubescent ardor.

The man says something. In a moment Leo would have acted. Rae reaches out, though. Her hand moves to the man's ear—most simple of acts. She withdraws a bill, ten dollars, crisp and unfolded. "Mine," she says. "You have my money. How did you get it?" The bill, you see, has her name scrawled in red ink on the corner. Rae, it says. That turns the man from Leo and Molly. He squints. "I know who the hell you are," he says. "You're that damn trickster."

Interesting how that word is used—a curse, an insult, a demeaning description. But Rae now rises, smiles, nods, bows. Trickster. Yes, trickster.

Molly is annoyed because people are watching. She doesn't like this turn of attention. Leo is very amused. Hey, he says. Hey.

31

The recording is old. A scratch right after Heifetz bows down. Rae doesn't know how the scratch happened. Max Bruch's *Scottish Fantasy*. Very fond of that. Now the phonograph—nothing hi-fi about that. Still, the woman next door batters the wall, probably with her broom handle. Rae imagines that side of the wall scratched and nicked by these rams. The music isn't loud. The woman bangs out of anger. She has a daughter—a pretty child, girl of about twelve. The mother brought her to Rae three years ago. Knocks on her door uninvited. Listen to this, the woman says. You got to hear this.

The child was dressed in blood-red tights and gauzy over-skirt— a net spangled with a tangle of beads. The child went on point and twirled. "My desert is calling," the child wailed. From Sigmund Romberg, the mother says. Isn't she something? She deserves a chance in the movies, television. Use her—put her on. Rae tells the woman that children do not perform on her show. Not that kind of show. She would have tickets sent, though— two. They could be in the audience. The woman says, I don't need you for tickets. Who needs you for tickets? Don't do me any favors!

Now, she torments Rae's wall.

Everybody has twelve blocks in their life. This, Rae heard from Carrie. And within this area most of a life is lived. Who belongs within these blocks? Sometimes, not who you'd expect.

It rains all day Monday. Los Angeles is never comfortable with rain. Rae knows a sociologist who insists that rain in L.A. makes people crazy. She has a meteorological chart cross-referenced to disasters. Murders, for instance. Twelve to one on rainy days, she swears.

Leo comes to lunch at one. Come over to my place, Rae insists. I'll bring in some deli—potato knishes, dill pickles. Name your favorite beer. Leo protests slightly. It was his invitation, and he had suggested two, three restaurants. Restaurants where you could be seen and the food is careful artistry. Rae says no.

She lives a block off Fairfax. She never invited Leo before. Look, they are friends—but old friends. Shared memories, not a shared present. Leo hasn't been there before, but Rae is not good about entertaining. She figures he will be prompt. No reason not to be—no one to see, no one to impress. At five past one he rings the bell.

"So this is where you hide," he says. He walks right past Rae and then from room to room—four. The kitchen is large, the cabinets need repainting.

"You are kidding?" he says. "You must be kidding. I'll be damned. You know what you have done? A duplicate of the old apartment in Washington Heights, isn't it? Sure, it is."

He walks over to the kitchen table, heavy oak. He rubs the edge. "My God, I remember this table. Look, here's the silverware drawer—it cuts your knees if you sit on that side. Your grandmother's furniture. Don't tell me you paid to have it shipped to L.A.? Were you nuts? This gives me the chills. I hate anything from back then. Why did you do this?"

Rae shrugs. "No hidden reason—you think I had a hidden reason? The stuff was in storage for years, decades. I paid the storage. I was moving into this apartment, I called the company. Ship, I said. Filled the rooms—I was furnished. Sit down, we'll eat."

On the kitchen table—the silverware drawer side—Rae has arranged a platter of corned beef and pastrami, edged with slices of tongue. Caraway-seeded rye bread, roughly cut. A trembling embankment of pickles. Moist pepper-speckled coleslaw, potato salad sprinkled with Hungarian paprika.

Now, in her kitchen—the kitchen in Los Angeles—Leo pulls a chair up to the table. Leo bites into a sandwich. Rae, too. Both of them have strong appetites.

"Do you know," Leo says and wags a quarter of a pickle at Rae. Caraway seeds outline his gums. "Do you know that I sat at this very table—when? Must be my third year in college. You dance up to me, flick my arm with a dishcloth. You're going to California, Leo. That's where you're going. Out of a clear blue sky—you said that."

"I did not."

"Absolutely."

"Well, I could have just as well sent you to Florida or Timbuktu."

"In a pig's eye—California, you said. Weird."

"I made a joke back there—you probably mentioned California to me. You probably did. So forget it. How are you, anyway? How's Molly?"

"Who?"

"Molly."

"I don't know. Anyway, life is all right. Maybe all right."

"Yeah. How's your kids—Claude and Erica?"

"Fine, fine. In Connecticut."

"With their mother—Linda?"

"Come right out and ask—you want to know details? Well, she left me. Simple as that—forget the newspapers. You know how I met Linda? I met her out here. She came to visit her brother. He's a bozo, so forget him. I met her, a prima donna, a wondrous woman. A wondrous woman—cool and proper, though moody. Then one day—should I have expected it? Sure. One day she tells me she met someone. He's young, he's charming, he loves her. It isn't a scandal—I say go. She goes."

"She married him yet?"

"Not yet. You want to hear something? I immediately thought when I first saw Linda that she could have paired with that guy you married—what's-his-name. Perfect match."

"Yes."

32

"Lila, it's me. Hell, I am sorry, about the time difference. Don't tell me what time it is—listen. I'm marrying. Yes, again."

"My God, do you know what time it is? Who?"

"You won't guess. You can't guess. I'm marrying Leo."

"Who?"

"Leo Littweiler."

"You're kidding?"

"No, I am not. We have fun together, Lila. I mean we laugh, we joke, we have a good time. We eat the same foods. Our memories collide."

"Think this through, Rae. Fun is one thing, marriage is another. Believe me—I know what I am talking about."

"We should have done this sooner," Leo says. "Want another slice of pizza? I really enjoy eating pizza in bed."

"Yes, another slice. And more wine. I love eating in bed. Really do."

"Yeah—I have this problem, Rae. I suddenly have this dumb problem—it came up today."

"What?"

"A telephone call. Linda—all tears. It's over, she says. It was stupid, she says. It was physical. Rae, Linda wants to come back and with the kids."

"That's impossible—we are married. You and I are married. Fourteen months—yes, fourteen."

"I know. She says the kids miss me."

"Listen, Leo, I have been thinking anyway about going back East."

"Powell won't like that."

"Fuck him."

Powell has a corner office. He says to Leo Littweiler, "One day she'll dry up and that will be the end of this. And we'll have invested what? Fortunes. What kind of shit is this anyway—the show lives in her head. What the hell is that?"

In this office, with its gray-and-blue-striped Edward Fields carpet, are two large ficus trees placed at an angle to the windows. They ought to live, the light is good, and the woman who tended them was conscientious, although Powell had her fired last month. Still, the trees never flourished. But they belong in that corner, they fit there. The greenhouse sent up palms, dieffenbachia, crowns of thorns. They don't look right. Anyway, they die, too. Every time the dying plants are removed, Powell is conscious of a bare space. He won't have artificial, no matter how good.

Every three months the greenhouse sends up new trees. It is a business expense, but Powell resents it. Two hundred-fifty dollars every three months. Powell's neckties average about seventy-five dollars each. Sometimes he splatters them with oil from salad, or he grows excited and waves his fork and sauce from pasta flies upward. Last week he threw away three neckties. He thought of them as not quite two trees.

"Leave Rae alone," Leo says. "It works, don't fix it."

"Spare me," Powell says, "your Talmudic sayings. Fix it? She's a head case. The only question is how far. Tell me that, Leo— how far? Nothing on paper. No one knows what she'll do or say. And in front of kids—it could explode."

Leo steps back and bumps against a tree. Leaves scatter at the blow. Autumn in the office. "Damn trees," Powell says. "I'll change florists again."

"Leave her alone," Leo says. "I know Rae—we'll lose her otherwise."

Powell glares, kicks a tub of earth. He can't lose her right now. She's hot.

———

It is Rae's conjurer's look, the practiced smile, the eyes focused on the distance—in this case, the knob of a cabinet in the apartment she shares with Leo. "Tell Powell that no trees will ever grow in his room—in that office. Ever," Rae says.

Leo wipes his neck. The air conditioning is set too low for his taste. "Why the hell did you say that? That's what I mean, Rae. Trees—Powell was bitching about the trees in his office just this morning."

"You think it's magic?" Rae says. "Don't tell me you really believe that. It's tricks, Leo. All tricks. But *my* tricks. Don't forget. There is only one Miz Magic. Tell Powell that. One thing I know for certain—Powell is not in the twelve blocks of my life."

"What?"

G. I. Rosencantz
Sunshine Publishing Co.
Oleana, Fla. 33546–1075

Dear Mr. Rosencantz:

I definitely sniff a rat. This is re the telephone call I received from my sister, Lila (Dr. Lila Howard). She has been contacted by a man named Gregory (no last name). Gregory wants to ask questions about Miz Magic. Doing research, he says. Lila is uncertain whether it was for an article or a broadcast. Anyway, he calls—he exists.

Now I am aware that I may not have given you the "dirt" you want—but I will. Perhaps I am looking in the wrong direction. Maybe Rae stole some of her tricks—her magic. That's possible. Maybe there's some behind-the-scenes power struggle.

But this is my story—I'll do it. So, Mr. Rosencantz, call off your dog(s).

Yours truly,
Carolyn Howard

Carolyn Howard
Box 117
Crosby Falls, N.Y. 11172

Dear Ms. Howard:

You better move your _____ or someone else will tell the
truth about Rae Howard. I don't know who this Gregory is, but
apparently he's doing something. Forget the stolen tricks or the
power stuff. Real secrets about women are always sexual. Remember that.

Yours,
G. I. Rosencantz

35

"Lila, what don't I know? After Rae divorces Leo, she returns to
New York, she meets Peter again and marries him. It can't truly
be that way: Enter the happy wife and stepmother."

"Why can't it?"

"I believe that she is hiding something. Would you say that
Rae is an honest person?"

"For God's sake, Carrie, you know her as well as I do. Anyway,
it's my experience that what is most concealed, well, is erotic in
nature, particularly for women."

"Sexual secrets are already under consideration. You don't think
that anything in her background that is tricky could involve her
career? Not that magic is truly a career."

"No, I don't."

"Lila, sisters are more than cousins. You know how much this
means to me. If Rae ever told you anything, you would tell me,
wouldn't you? I need help, Lila. As one sister to another."

"I know Rae as well as you do. Look—I don't know what to
say. How about Peter? Try an approach to him."

"Peter? You are joking. He's still married to Rae and besides—I cannot stand him."

"Then go with what you have. You know, maybe, 'Is Miz Magic a Role Model?'"

"Don't be absurd. There's a secret. And someone else is looking, too. If I had any doubts—the presence of someone else confirms my original idea. I have to look harder, that's all."

Part II

◆

"I tell you, every audience loves to see a woman sawed in half. Rather primitive, isn't it?"

—P. T. Selbit, 1902
(reported conversation with
impresario A. L. Parker)

G. I. Rosencantz
Sunshine
Oleana, FL

Attention Rosencantz:

It has come to my attention that you and your scumbag publication are planning to do a story about me. I'll sue the pants off you! Don't think I won't. Bear this in mind—you *putz!*

Anyway, why do people always want to get you? The "you" is generic. But they do. Statistically, I think they go after women more than men. (You can take this idea, if you want it.) What's terrible is that it isn't only men after you—it is women, too. Get back, they say. Get down. Be like us. Whatever the "us" is.

Yours (in total disgust),
Raemunde Howard

P.S. If it turns out to be true that your source is my cousin Carrie Howard, you can be certain your facts won't stand up anywhere. I am exactly who I seem to be.

1

My life on parade, my life on display. My life. What do they know? Vera is always chanting how my public has rights. Rights! They have rights to a good trick—and that's it.

I don't know why they have to know about me. Why should they? I can see Carrie dredging up everything. But—and most important—only her version of everything. Listen, if there was one thing I learned young, it was what to say and what not to say. I learned that from my father. His profession made him secretive. But that was useful training for a child. If they don't ask, he said to me, don't tell them. Keep your memories clipped and pruned. That's what I did.

Now I won't say that nothing is known. After all, we spent a lot of time together. Some memories must commingle. The three of us. Carrie and Lila and Rae. A bloody triptych.

This is what we know about each other. I once heard Lila gush at a man: "Everything," she said. "I know everything about her." She wasn't trying to sound important; she wanted the man to love her.

Carrie said that we met at a crucial point in our lives. I think that we were fully made by the time we met. Our babyhood spent in different wombs.

Carrie wept and wept—yes, it was in my arms. A man named Wesley, so Christian, so worthy, was leaving. He was an artist and although his paintings can now be bought, it pleases me that they are ordinary pictures. I took Carrie to the gallery on Fifty-ninth. See, I said. He is a salon painter. He does the perfection of unreality. All Carrie did was clutch her arms. We went away. She had had his child. She waited too long—certain that he would appear. She told him, and he didn't come. She went to the Edith C. Clinton Home and signed for adoption. None of us ever saw that baby girl. Lila said it was for the best. She could be right. Afterward, Carrie came back to New York and went to bed for three months.

Lila is married to Melvin. He is an alcoholic, she says solemnly. At least twice a year he is locked up in a hospital where he has the DTs and soaks his sheets in urine. He displays symptoms of Korsakoff's psychosis. Carrie screams at Lila on the telephone: "He's a goddamn drunk. A drunk! You are wasting your life on a drunk." Lila has been married to Melvin for fourteen years. Carrie and I believe that she doesn't sleep with him more than two months in a year.

Lila was the one who said I should learn to do something. Learn something for which someday I could be paid a salary.

Carrie and Lila remember me at different times in my life. No one else knew me through all those times. I was in love with Whalen Clarke, and they knew me then. It was Lila who warned me. He's not just a WASP, she said. He's the supreme goy, Rae. He'll cheat and cheat. He won't even be able to help it—he's that gorgeous.

Carrie caught the bouquet at that wedding.

They knew Leo, but they weren't present when I married him. It was an informal wedding. Leo and I thought that was fun. Like a joke wedding performed in a professional wedding chapel— everything reusable.

Lila and Carrie were by my side when I married Peter. I had a corsage—it is absurd to throw a corsage.

They weren't always there. What should I say? I think that lives are the business of the people who own them. And it is not simple—a case of my memories versus their memories. No logic when you traverse memories. For instance, they swear certain nights never happened. I know different.

But let me tell you—Do you think Carrie knows my earliest memories? What does she offer as truth? A harangue of misread clues, a furious passion for unproven insights. Carrie does not know my earliest memories.

Those early memories. Hasty thoughts, scraps of being, sublime optimism.

My bubbaloo, Nat said to me. My lollipop. What's that? Watch, Nat, I said. (Did I have a baby lisp?) Watch, daddyoh. Here are three cups—one ball. See, poppo. I'm gonna put this ball under a cup. Keep watching. Now I move the cups, keep watching. Uh-one, uh-two, uh-three. Which cup has the ball? Guess, Nat. Guess. This one. Wrong. Look—it's here. Keep watching. I'm gonna do it again.

2

This is how I knew I was famous. I was walking up Forty-sixth Street where it crosses the Avenue of the Americas. A boy tried to pull away from his mother's hand. "Look, look," he yelled. "It's Miz Magic."

"It is not," his mother said; she was upset. It was wet, the street held a slushy tide, rivulets of icy water drifted across her boots. "And don't you pull away like that again."

"It is! It is! Miz Magic!"

I reached out with my hand. "Yes, it's me."

"Get away from us," the woman hissed.

3

This is about character assassination. Forget murder or adultery or embezzlement. These can be overcome. You think not? The streets are filled with resurrected presidents, murderers, adulterers, and embezzlers. They are public figures—forgiven and grown newly respectable. They sit at your dinner table and explain how they were truly sorry—things just happen.

But pure and simple character assassination—the gossipy, the smarmy—that's what gets you. The important thing is not to have a secret. It is secrets that they want. If you confess first, that takes all the fun out of it.

The best attempt at character assassination was by a woman named Gwendolyn who rummaged through the layers of my life. What could she find? She couldn't shout to the world that your children watch a thrice-married woman. I went on a talk show— it was before Oprah Winfrey asked—and I told about my marriages. I sat up there wearing a newly purchased Liz Claiborne shirtwaist dress that I was told added respectability without maturity. I explained to the worried mothers of America that, yes, I had been married three times. I lit the air with the fluorescence of truth. I did the routine of first husband (married too soon); second husband (married too fast)—and now the third and final husband. How long ago was that? Peter and I were married two years. Five years ago.

And we bonded, me and the mothers of America. So many among them had followed my path to one degree or another. And I did my laugh line: "Isn't it wonderful that I found three men to marry me—and they say you have to be pretty."

In a way, I am an American baby-sitter. Your kids are safe with me. Sit them down, turn on the telly, here she comes. Miz Magic!

Ah, but to return to character assassination. That woman, Gwendolyn, found zilch—the big zero. If you are careful, all they get are the facts. Those snips and snaps of my myth hardly compared with "Woman Has Three Heads"—pictures on page 3. Or "Lady Flies Around Room"—documentation to follow.

I cooperated. Well, why not. I figured that they knew their business. They had researchers—Gwen had two. I thought maybe they could locate people whom I hadn't seen in years. I thought maybe they could find my father, Nat, or my stepmother, Smyrna. But they didn't.

What I have now is this new spook. On the other hand, it could be my generic Mad Fan. It happens from time to time. Telephone calls, being followed. My husband, Peter, says I overreact.

Actually, I was less worried by the calls than surprised by the ability of the caller to zero in so effectively. What was the purpose? Someone must have an assignment. I could find my picture on the cover of whatever was most lurid that month.

What I decided is that I won't ask the new spook to find Nat. If you want to find your father, you should look yourself.

4

Carrie is my cousin. People used to say that Carrie and Lila and Rae were like sisters. But we weren't—we were like cousins. Lila told me that when I was living in California Carrie got sick and tired of feminism and causes. All causes, she said. She had folded notices; she had marched; she had torn off opposing posters. Anyway, nothing had changed for her. She still made supper for Dunstead. She still washed the kids' clothes. What had it got her? She was going to take care of herself for a change.

Carrie went back to college and studied journalism. God knows why, Lila said, I always thought she wanted to draw or paint. She was terrific in fashion. Afterward, Carrie did the occasional feature for her town newspaper. She told me that she was wasting her time, Lila said. But then there was that incident with the minister and the fourteen-year-old. Carrie was there—the man lived six, seven blocks away. She got that story and it was picked up by a service. That's how she got the opportunity, Lila said.

Carrie called me. Now her voice wasn't nervous. It was remote, controlled. "I'm going to do an article on you," she said. "Maybe a book—but certainly an article."

"What? About the show?"

"No, about you. I'll be up front, Rae. You may not like it—I'm going to dig and tell the truth."

"What truth? And why me? Tell me that, why me?"

"Because I don't know anyone else, that's why. I know you. And they're giving me a chance. I have an assignment, I have expense money."

"My God, you want to create a scandal. Is that what you want, Carrie?"

"Yes."

"You don't know the hell about me."

"You got to be kidding. We grew up together! You think I don't know about you?"

"Well, then I guess this is the end."

"The end of you, maybe. The beginning of me."

I called Lila. I didn't know how things were between her and Carrie. They are sisters—blood sisters.

"I can't believe this," I said.

"She's going to do it. Look, I tried to talk her out of it. She told me to keep my therapeutic crap to myself."

"What started it?"

"You did, Rae. That announcement you put into the AFL-CIO newsletters about looking for Nathaniel Howard. She called me up—Rae is looking for Uncle Nat, she said. We knew it was you— who else is called Raemunde. She figured it meant something. So she contacted some scandal rag located in the south. And after the reverend and the fourteen-year-old, they said go ahead."

"There's nothing to find."

"That's what I told her," Lila said. "We know each other's lives completely."

"Yes, we do."

5

I remember this and believe that it happened. I see Nat sitting at the table. I am prancing around trying to keep his attention. I realize now that his smile is indulgent. I am seven years old and know that it is very difficult to keep his attention. Every few minutes, he turns away. I wave my hands. I didn't understand the proper daddy-daughter ploys, and he slips from me. But I knew even then how much more effective it would have been to have been pretty.

I have no pictures of Nat. All the papers are gone, too. His full name is Nathaniel Howard. The last day I saw him was on January 10, 1963. That was two days before my birthday, and Nat had bought me a white blouse with a Peter Pan collar edged with a quarter inch of crocheted hearts. I suspect he went into a store and told the saleswoman that his daughter was going to be eleven and what did she have. I had given him a list. I wanted two packs of cards, bridge size; a square silk scarf, pattern unimportant; and a package of threepenny nails.

I think of Nat as being in the forefront of a trend—the vanishing American father. The father of my cousins Lila and Carrie is buried in Long Island. At our first meeting they said their father was away. I misunderstood. His name was Laurence Howard; he was Nat's brother. He got up from the dinner table, his daughter said. I have a choking feeling in my throat, he told them. Lila said that my father is probably dead, too. I said no. I don't believe she meant to hurt me.

I can see Nat in a room somewhere. I make his hair gray. He is a tall, thin man wearing a flannel shirt and jeans. I change the room. Make it a bar. A cloud of smoke but no more than two, three people. The television is on. The set rests on one of those frames screwed into the wall. That's my daughter, Nat says, turning to those others—the two or three men. Really, he says. That's my daughter, I swear, he says. That's her—Miz Magic. The men don't believe him. My daughter, he insists. They change the channel; they don't want to see me.

What I would like Nat to know is that he could actually come back. I would like to see him. We could talk. He could explain to me what the terrible thing was that sent him away and kept him away. Lila and Carrie tell me that I'm a damn fool. He should rot, they say.

I wave my hands. Still, the bartender changes the channel. They are too old to watch Raemunde Howard. I would like to yell: I forgive! But they are in the middle of a ball game.

6

Here's something else Carrie doesn't know, because I never told her. How I got my name. I was named after a full-length slip, bust 34, peach-colored. I learned that when I was nine years old. Rummaging in a shoe box—could be labeled Treasures of the Family—I found a rectangle of pasteboard caught between the fingers of a single glove. Souvenir, talisman, omen. Thick black Gothic letters on a silver background: *"Raemunde—Lingerie of Distinction."* Stamped on the back were the particulars of the garment and style number. Style #423.

"What the hell were you doing in those things," Smyrna says. But too late.

That was me. Raemunde. I had always thought my name belonged to an ancestor—mysterious woman, maybe two, three generations back. My stepmother, Smyrna, never said. But I had seen that name as linkage—dressed my ancestor in dark green velvet, with a white square collar of lace.

Raemunde, then, was the name of a moment. Raemunde. Teachers never liked the name. Heathenish sound—pronounced the word at tongue's length. *Ray-mund-day.* Put in that extra *d.* But after my revelation, it was no longer necessary to protect the name. Call me Rae, I said. That school was amiable. It was a time of Marys and Janes and Susans. For scenery, we had the smoke-stacks of South Chicago.

Afterward, whenever we moved I kept the Rae. Raemunde, you see, had no roots and could be shortened or lengthened at will. And ours was an American family of movers. Every city that knew me as Rae changed—and I was never there to bear witness. In Milwaukee, we lived off Center Street. Whenever I mentioned what I remembered—for instance, the tiny railroad bridge or the bottle factory—someone from that city would shake his head. No, someone would say, it's not like that at all. The hill on the corner of Fifty-first Street had been planed down. The school named after a mayor gone. In St. Louis, we lived on Delmar Boulevard, several blocks from the corners where stone lions guarded the entrance to U. City. We lived above a real-estate office. Four rooms. I dreamed of houses. Smyrna snorted. If we lived over a bank, she said, would you dream of money?

Nothing was the same in any of those cities when I saw them again—not Chicago or Milwaukee or St. Louis. Or dark little towns off rural routes.

We were a secretive family. Individual secrets. My father worked for a union. What he did, he never said. Smyrna one day bleached her yellow hair a shocking white-blonde. Then she bleached mine. If it was a disguise, it didn't work. No children had hair like that. Not down the streets where we lived. You look like a circus pony, a teacher said. I told Smyrna. That was a mistake. She came to school and raged until the teacher's lips grew thin and parched. Later, I paid for that.

Sometimes a woman lived with us. I was told to call her Aunt Dee. She had a diamond ring and a boyfriend named Fred. Every-one I knew had names that you could remember and say easily. My father's name was Nat.

But I was first Raemunde. Then Rae. Plain Rae. My hair was wild and brown—the blonde cut away as it grew longer. There were things I was willing to try, but I lacked the talents. Was I kissable? Even if I pressed purple lipstick stolen from the five-and-dime onto my lips, I was not chosen. I knew three girls born to be kissed and felt up in back rooms.

We moved one night. Moved at midnight. Smyrna says our name now ends in the letters *ar*. Forget the *d*. "Never," I say. "Yes, it does," she says with fierce ardor. "And don't you forget that!"

In the new school, I had no past. One evening, Smyrna took me to a show at the union hall. A show for children. An Easter show. There was a singer—a woman with a lollipop face—two boys who tap-danced, a creature in a rabbit's costume, and a magician named Jim Haw the Great. My memory was always good. He was a true magician—worthy of finer places than that drafty hall with cracked plaster and coldly determined people. But he had fallen on difficult days—he did his act in a sweater against the cold. Shabby, even for us. Oh, but he was good; he did the Malini's Blindfold Card-Stabbing Trick, the cut rope, the vanishing scarf. Afterward, the children grouped around the players, the show over. The rabbit had the audience, because he gave out bags of jelly beans; even the singer attracted some admirers in her spangled golden dress. But I went straight for Jim Haw. That was terrific, I said. Best thing here. Best ever. The man gave me a bear hug, a hug rich in scents of wool and whiskey. How'd you do it? I said. Do what? I was clever. Ask for everything—get nothing. I made a modest reply. Just the switched coin in the ear.

He showed me. See, he said. He showed me how to hide the coin under my collar, how to switch from left to right hand. The fingers graceful. I had the slim hands of my father. Long tapered fingers. Try, Jim said. I took the coin. I had watched. It slid easily from fingers to fingers. I pulled it off. Hey, he said and applauded. It was that: a success. Approval and then success.

That can start you on a path. I soon did coins behind ears on a regular basis. Added the cat's cradle. The cigarette from the nose. Here, Rae, others called. Pull a coin out. Flushed with joy, I did. I developed a patter, became stagestruck. Jokes and tricks.

Rae wasn't so bad. Rae was always good for a laugh. Sometimes I did these tricks with dramatic flourishes. Then I would be "Raemunde the Great" or "Raemunde, the Woman of Mystery."

Now would I have taken this path if I had been Alice or Susan or Elizabeth? Hard to say. But I was Rae—formed by my name, made by my name.

7

What I suppose I keep trying to come back to is the fact that my life is like anyone else's. I defy Carrie to say otherwise. Let me speak about the day I realized I loved Peter, my husband. I believe that such days exist for people—days when they realize love.

Something scared me. A sharp bile taste, a panicky foreboding. I tried to place the feeling, to give it a site and a reason. Made it tension, an untrustworthy déjà vu embedded in my mind. What else could it have been? I was not a mountebank, a charlatan— any ghosts that I ever used were of my making. Yet for an uncommon instant I believed that I knew that the man—the one in the expensive beige polo coat—was going to fall. And that, of course, was ridiculous—my thought and the act must have merely crossed. Perhaps it was the drama of the situation. But it made me pause, and thus I wasn't quick enough. The man was young—that gave the scene its strangeness. A young, prime-of-life man, with his lips gone tight, one hand rising up in a theatrical flourish to clutch at the wide knot of the perfect tie. The fingers of the other hand straightened; a folded newspaper dropped. It was then that both hands went to his chest, pushing back the lapels of the coat. He said nothing, nothing audible, no squawk, no yell, no shivering moan. As if rehearsed, the man collapsed onto the platform floor, a soundless bending of the knees, an unbroken downward drift. The drop, though, was so swift that no one could have reached him.

A woman screamed, one of those embarrassed sounds choked off before it had a chance to echo. Someone yelled, "Christ! Get the token seller." Not unreasonable, for authority must lie some-where. A student carrying a large canvas bag ran back up the stairs from the subway platform. "I'll get help," he shouted. "Don't worry!"

Now here is where powers of attention come into play, and not some nonsense of clairvoyance. If I assume that I knew he was going to fall. How? Perhaps I saw a muscular twitch, noticed him rub his arm, heard him clear his throat of the strangle of catarrh. Those were events I could have registered, stored in memory.

Presto, I know then that he will fall.

It was seconds—only seconds. During this time, I am still con-fused by my sense of having known what will occur.

Another train arrives on the express track. Exiting passengers carefully skirt the man. A new arrival—waiting like me for the local—comes forward. She wears a long, loose coat, very stylish. Careless of the cascade of wool on the gray concrete, she squats near the man, touches his neck. Then she takes a handkerchief. I saw it. A *silk*—a specially prepared handkerchief for magic. The woman bears the badge of respectability—her face carries the samaritan's expression. Her hand with its good-wifely band of gold. Gently, she wipes the man's face. Of what? Sweat? Pain? It was a good distraction, the way she shook her head. He must be dead, a voice whispers. Dead? another responds.

The handkerchief floats across the man's chest as she loosens his necktie. How kind. Then, with a skillful, graceful swoop, she gathers up the handkerchief and the thick waves of her coat and stands up.

The *silk*, of course, carries the wallet—in its unseen pocket. On the local track a train arrives screeching and howling into the station, and the woman departs on it. A perfect crime.

The original participants in the event are gone except for me. A man comes forward—not one suitable for kind gestures, but not quite a vagrant. The new people who wait look disturbed. They stare at the man lying on the platform, at the fine cordovan oxfords on his feet. The new helper wears a sweater, frayed at the elbows. He, too, squats by the body. He is better than I would have expected. "Hey, buddy," he says. "Hey, buddy, you all right?" Words make you look at the man's face. Hands only lightly touch the body. When the man stands up, he has the watch. Nothing special—just basic palming. Good enough for this audience. But mustn't linger. Surely a cop would be on the way. The man was up, moving backward, careful not to run or even to disappear. Not yet.

I was all right now. Poor oaf—without either wallet or watch. The watch made the journey from hand to new owner's pocket. The thief didn't even touch it again. Good, smart. Fumble with your fingers in a pocket, you look nervous. Ah, another train— local track.

Collapsed man on the platform must be responsible for the sudden shortage of express trains. Everyone late. There he was— the watch man—short, dark hair. The little *bossoletino!* He's planning on riding that train downtown. Get off at Twenty-third. Walk to his fence. How much? Rolex, maybe. The man moves, I move. I'm good, good. I'm the best. I don't even brush against him. My fingers are warm, lubricated by ball-squeezes. No nails— no click, no pinch. Bingo, I have the watch. The man is on the train; first dark tunnel, his hand will go into that pocket with its astonishing emptiness, searching then for a hole, looking like any subway-train masturbator. Incredulous then. Who did it? Will he guess me? That woman with thick hair pinned up, jeans, high heels, tight shirt. Showy—makes you nervous to even talk to her. No, lost it. He'll think that. Dropped it just before the doors shut. It could have fallen onto the tracks, annealed and made one with those tracks by now. A flattened blob of metal. Well, never mind. Another one will come along.

I kneel now. My turn. What's she want? She cannot be trusted. See me. All I do is place fingers on the man's forehead. "Croaked," I say. "Surely croaked." No one expects it, so the watch goes back on his wrist, two fingers seal it. Maybe the watch was engraved on the back. Maybe it said *"J. L. with love A. M."*

This is not a record of knowing what will happen. I have never known what will happen.

Peter sits at a table in an Italian restaurant on Eighth Avenue. I am late because I waited on the subway platform. Doing what? Guarding the man. For three months—whenever I am in New York—Peter and I meet. How did it happen? Polly Jacobs brought him over at a party. "Peter Anson says he knows you," she said in disbelief. "From L.A." So we were re-introduced. I didn't think he understood a thing about magic. No, he didn't. But his daughter, he thought his daughter watched me. The lady magician.

It is amazing how warm and contented Peter could make me feel. He is sitting at that table, waiting—I see the single flower he has brought for me. He says I am so different from the women he meets who complain or fuss or make arch comments.

I was starting to worry, he says, rising as I approach the table.

So I tell him about the man on the platform. Do I mention my feeling? That absurd sense of *knowing*. I am talking on and on about what happened, about the woman and the wallet, about the man and the watch.

Quite suddenly Peter puts his hand gently over my lips. "Be still," he says. "I want to take care of you, Rae. I want to be the person you come to with problems. I love you—and I thought I was finished with this—will you marry me?"

Brim full of sexual desire, we cling to each other, we embrace. We spend the night together. And during that time—not anticipated by me—we are totally in rapture.

The next morning I telephone Carrie, and then Lila. Love, I tell them, at last.

Sometimes I wake up—not from a bad dream; simply wake up and wonder how I got here. Which is a kind of bad child's joke— the one that begins: How did I get here?—that elicits a physiological explanation of life. And all the poor kid wanted to know was how he got *here*.

How I got here.

When Peter said he wanted to move out of the city, it was a time of great love. We giggled over what he called the ordinariness of our passion. For we cannot bear to be out of each other's sight. In that silly apartment, three and a half rooms, drafty, scented by disinfectants, we made love, had our dinners delivered, and feasted on spaghetti, or orange-flavored chicken, or chilled steak in the bedroom.

Then we married. I wore a corsage of waxy camellias, and we went to spend a month on the Cape. Then one day—for that's the way things happen—the faucet in the kitchen broke off and water spurted over Peter's clothes. He had to teach. Look at him now! The laundry had not been picked up. The man next door started a twenty-four-hour marathon of reggae. Unmistakable odors of decadence permeate the machinery of the Otis elevator.

Peter said we had to move out of the city. And that even if we hadn't married, he would want to move out of the city. He said that if he sees one more city roach that you could put a bridle on, or if he hears one more shrieking declaration of hate through the wall or down from the ceiling, he would go mad. Furthermore, there were the children to consider. They are his children, who come like visiting waifs to sob and soil their sleeping bags.

The problem is—I was so busy. I spent five days a week at the studio. Sometimes the day ended at eight P.M. Go ahead, I told Peter. Not that he needed my blessing. He taught on Tuesdays and Thursdays. He vowed to take a hiatus from his work and devote himself to the search.

Real-estate sections of the newspaper are suddenly everywhere. Marked and circled. Towns acceptable and towns not. Peter is wooed by real-estate agents and receives mysterious messages from a series of first-name-only ladies. They drive him everywhere.

While small children cavort around the legs of Miz Magic, Peter finds the house in Berdan. I located the place, sweetheart, he says. And with enthusiasm and affection, Peter drives me to see Berdan. I am truly charmed. Broad streets, trees, grass.

He wasn't trying to be a snob or elitist, he said. But Berdan's community could offer what we needed. There were the shop-keepers who worked and lived in the commercial part of town. The Irish, in the area for more than one hundred years, occupied and seemed confined to the southern end of the town. On the lovely hills grew the large, the expensive homes. Peter explained that, despite this unfortunate stratification, it is the sort of place, the sort of neighborhood, where we could expect to be left alone. Where we could be known as simply Peter and Rae.

As for the house, it was perfect—neither too close to the city nor too much in the country. Peter wanted space, he wanted privacy, but he isn't searching for property that looked as if you ought to keep horses or cultivate a field. The naming of the roads. Some things can't be helped. The house was on Hawthorne Road between Emerson and Melville. The truth was—I kissed Peter—if he wanted it, I wanted it, too. We raced across the lawn; it was like being back in those three and a half rooms.

His choice was almost a bargain—an estate sale. A family gone berserk in time, a marriage of cousins, an embezzlement, a vanished will. The only sister left of the original family lives on the West Coast. The house, designed by Turnbull, was built in 1936. Peter never thought that he would want to live in a structure that outwardly conventional. His taste ran to Frank Lloyd Wright.

But he has done research. Turnbull had vision. Maybe it was a vision that turned back into the past—but certainly vision. In a time of cheap workmen, mantels were carved and copied from photographs. Here a touch from Hadrian's villa at Tivoli. There a cathedral window. The entry is a variation of *le style ogival.* Rare woods line the doorways. All this, Peter pointed out to me. No one, Peter assured me, could afford this detailing today, even if the craftsmen were available. And it wasn't too big. It was a house where people could live. So we bought it.

On the second day after the moving van departed, a large, a truly ostentatious basket of flowers was delivered. Stapled across the handle was a red ribbon and on the ribbon—written with a pen that emitted silver sparkles instead of ink—"Berdan Welcomes Miz Magic."

Peter was furious. Then it turned out that the basket was sent by the Association of Merchants. He calmed down. Afterward, we were Peter and Rae. Sometimes I was called Mrs. Anson.

We bought the *pied-à-terre* the year of the big snowstorm. For two days I was stranded in the city. I couldn't reach Berdan. Peter said we needed a place in the city. So we got one. Two and a half rooms that face Central Park. Peter anticipates the children wanting to use the apartment someday. Not now—now they are too young to stay alone in the city.

8

I remember being sick. Every child gets sick. But I am probably on my way to recovery, for I am bickering, finding fault with everything, with the bowls of thin soup, with the hair on my neck, with the weight of the quilt. Still, there were moments of fever—yes, I must have been feverish, because I see Smyrna with an aura about her, as if her yellow hair has dissolved in a crown of vapor that rises above her head. Look at this, Smyrna is saying. Offering me an entertainment before the alcohol rub with its dreaded smell. Smyrna has tissue paper, smooth and crisp sheets. Probably from the folded pile on the closet shelf. Smyrna hums as she picks up the paper. She lifts and folds, twists and folds. I watch, but my legs move restlessly on the bed. And when Smyrna is finished, all she has is a neatly intertwined package of paper missing only a string. Is that it? I prepare an assault of complaint. But Smyrna, still humming, picks up one of the small rags not yet moistened with alcohol. Watch, she commands. Package of tissue on her palm is draped with a rag. It is a day for a garden, Smyrna says. Ah yes, a day for a garden. With a flourish, a waving gesture, she pulls off the rag. In her hand where once had been a folded package, a flower rises in full bloom, wide tissue petals. It hangs from a stiff tissue stem. I am incredulous; I raise myself on one elbow. Wow, I say. Show me how. After the rub, Smyrna says.

9

There was a time when my friend Leo really intended to make me into a fortune-teller. Not an astrologer. Someone with visions. But I was never willing, and I suppose that might even have magnified his interest.

I don't believe in magic as defined this way—adepts, Zorastrian hopes, oracles, dreams. At any rate, I made only four appearances as a fortune-teller, earned a total of three hundred and fifty dollars, and closed the door on that forever. Although I still get requests for tea leaves, tarot, or to throw I Ching. Some requests come rather tastelessly when I am an invited guest.

When Grandmother Minnie Howard died, I invited Leo Littweiler to the apartment. Carrie and Lila went with the rest of the family to the house of one of Minnie's sisters. I hardly knew that woman. Come after the funeral, I told Leo. Come then. Leo was probably my oldest friend.

For the longest time, my best friend was a girl named Elaine. She lived two doors down, but it was more than propinquity. I was a magician; she was a dancer. Where we differed—Elaine was experimental, I was not. Her mother was an accountant. She was a nice woman. Elaine's father was a gambler. He came and went. Her genes, Elaine's mother said later, are his. Elaine pulled her eyebrows out one day, and then the family hauled her off to Long Island "to rest." She took something, Minnie said. You can bet she took something.

I fix platters for our lunch. True, I cooked none of the food. Cholent with hillocks of barley, a shimmer of chopped chicken liver, *lokshen kugel,* peppery-edged pastrami, kasha varnitchkes, sweet peppers, coleslaw. It is a nostalgic meal, what we used to eat on Saturday afternoons. Like the food I would later feed him in L.A.

Too much for two people. Greed, lust, indulgence. I'll take some of that and that and that. Even setting the table seems odd. The first time I ever offered any real food to a guest in this apartment. Cups of coffee didn't count.

The table looks right—colorful. Impressively laden, a landscape of plenty. First I thought I couldn't eat with Leo in the dining room. The dining room belonged to feasts and celebrations. A full set of furniture—table, chairs, buffet, china cabinet. The wood much darkened from years of generously applied wax, although none recently.

Then I decide that this is a ceremony—after the funeral. A ceremony. What was needed was courage. The dining-room table has a decent white cloth, and in a moment of riotous endeavor I place the splendors of delicatessen and ready-made on Minnie Howard's absolutely best china, a pattern studded with roses and thorn-bearing stems. She would have died—or died again—if she had seen that. When had that china been used? Never in the span of my memory, and tomorrow Cousin Luba Seneschel, its inheritor, was coming with three strong packing cartons to take it all away.

The silverware, heavy British silver complete with hallmarks, would stay. Minnie must have forgotten it. I set the table with that silver, each fork designed for the oversized hand. I wondered what we could get for it. Service for twelve.

I decide not to change my clothes. I wasn't in black. I wore a navy blue dress. It has long sleeves. It is hot, a dress for decorum. Minnie's sisters wore black at the funeral, as did a few nieces. But there were prints. And a lot of short sleeves.

Leo arrives punctually at three, as requested. I am amazed when I open the door. He wears a suit. Navy blue. He carries a string-wrapped white box from a bakery. My God, he is making the official mourning call.

He kisses my cheek, hugs me. "I'm sorry, babe," he says. He looks past me. No one is there.

I answer the unspoken. "Only you," I say. "The rest of the kin are holding their wake in Queens."

"I'll be damned," Leo says. "You didn't go?"

"You noticed. I would be the uninvited. The guest for whom the door is not opened—or maybe a crack. *Capisce?*"

Leo hands me the box, takes off his jacket and tosses it on a chair, removes his tie. He sees the table through the doorway. He is a big eater.

"I saw the old lady once," he remembers. "Not so bad to die when you're old. I mean it could be worse."

"Yes," I agree.

"Let's eat," Leo says. The ceremony is over.

"Sure."

I watch him pile pastrami on bread, layer it with coleslaw and slathers of rich, golden mustard. He doesn't speak for a while.

"You rich now?" he asks finally.

"No," I say. I gesture. "We got this, though. As residents, this is ours. Six rent-controlled rooms—lifetime. Carrie, Lila, and me."

"She wasn't loaded then? No dough left?"

I begin to build a sandwich of my own.

"Beer?"

"In the refrigerator."

Leo gets up and comes back with two bottles.

I bite into my bread. "She left me the furniture. Cousin Aaron did the will. Her sisters got the jewelry—the pins, the diamond earrings, the rings. She left her insurance to the same Aaron for his long service. Cousin Luba has the dishes. Hadassah got some money. Carrie and Lila got the rest. Except for my two thousand. And the dishes for a cousin. I also got the car—the Ford, 1965, thirty-five thousand miles."

"She was a bitch, Rae," Leo says, shifting the food in his mouth. "I always told you she was a bitch. Now what happens?"

"What happens? Nothing happens."

"You're not going to stay here?"

"Of course I am. Why not?"

"It's like death, Rae, that's why not. You have talents."

"Really. Should I set myself up to be a fortune-teller?" I close my eyes. "I think I want to be married. Yes, I want to be married. Husband, kids, house—dog."

At that point I start to cry—which is quite strange, because I rarely cry. Leo comes around to my side of the table and pats my shoulder. Why do people pat shoulders? I weep and weep. He misunderstands.

"Yeah," he says, "it's all right. She was your grandmother."

"Excuse me," I say, and go into the bathroom, where I turn on the cold water and throw handfuls at my face. I am crying for those of my aspirations that do not seem possible.

When I return to the table, Leo is eating again.

"You need analysis," he says. "You remember Courtney? She went into analysis. Changed her."

"I'm going full time at Harter's Lumber," I say. "Starting Monday." I had been part-time in the back office for the past year. They liked me; they had been holding open the full-time position until I graduated.

"Well," Leo says. "To each his own. I can't wait to leave this city, Rae."

I knew he didn't get along with his parents—dour people who turned off lights. Leo invited me for dinner once. He told me the next morning that his mother said I wasn't suitable. Leo said that his parents wanted him to be taller. When they die, he told me, he would immediately join the Unitarian Church. I suspected that I wasn't going to see Leo again. Graduation was next Thursday. I suspected that this was it. He would go his way. I would stay behind in rent-controlled.

When I was part-time and a student, the other women at Harter's were friendly, I thought, but now I realized the difference. I had been outside and hadn't even known it. But as full-time, I belong and regularly eat lunch with Janet and Alice and Bebe. Harter's runs essentially two businesses. They have the slower-paced store part, for men who come in needing the plumber's helper or enough wood to repair the molding around the dining-room door. But Harter's also has big trucks that carried the heavy loads of lumber. They have contacts and connections. Occasionally, men with winter-bronzed faces and long overcoats appear to be shown into Mr. Harter's knotty-pine-paneled office. I learn, watching these arrivals, that loose, almost oversized overcoats convey power.

I tell Janet and Alice and Bebe about my desires—how I am trying to enhance my feminine side in preparation for marriage.

Janet shrugs. "Marriage?" she says. "You should only know."

Neither Alice nor Bebe contradicts her. But all agree that what I want is normal, commendable. When I was a student, they had thought of me as stuck-up—and a weird magic nut. That surprises me. But now they suggest that I dress too plain, that I need a permanent, and definitely need earrings. They fix me up with Janet's brother, who was a CPA and for whom a college girl is a requirement.

He took me to the movies, *Easy Rider,* he bought popcorn, and afterward, in his car, he plunged his hand down the front of my sweater. Those artificially buttered fingers, each with the faint rasp of dried husks, squeezed. I caught hold of his little finger and pulled it backward. He screamed; he actually screamed. A high-pitched, almost feminine scream. He said I was a fucking bitch. Janet was cool to me for a day or two, but she recovered.

They fixed me up with Alice's neighbor—a widower less hot to trot. I tried being docile, wore a high-necked blouse that buttoned in the back and was hell to put on, topped with a double strand of fake pearls around my neck. He was a nice man, sweet faced and sad. He told Alice that he had liked me but I was a half head taller than he was—he didn't think he could get used to that.

Soon afterward, I found an evening job in a bookstore in the Village. Needed extra money, I explained, for the dentist.

With two jobs I am successfully out of the dating market. I like the bookstore, no one bothers me. I can read magazines on my break, if I turn the pages carefully so that the magazines don't look read. For my birthday, I have my ears pierced by a girl in a white coat behind the jewelry counter at Goldmeir's Discount. Afterward, I regularly wear a pair of gold loop earrings. I know my life lacks sparkle. I am twenty years old. I need a plan.

The bookstore is having its employees' Christmas Party. The store closes at six P.M. on that Sunday. Five days before Christmas. None of the evening employees except for a manager and the cashier are regulars. The rest of us are part-time. We don't know each other very well either. There are a group of boys, students who are conversant with prime factors and group-analytic approaches and the strata of the earth's surface. Two other women work, depending on the evening—one is a theater major always being threatened for trying to light a cigarette in the storeroom. The other is political. She doesn't like me.

The party attracts a crowd. The unknown day people arrive. Some with dates or spouses. A few small children run wildly between Anthropology and Archaeology. A number of women take paper cups filled with punch to the section of Household Arts.

What happens is my fault. I am at the counter. There are pretzels—baked twigs shaped into circles. The lonely girl on the other side of the counter is perhaps ten—party-dressed in black velvet with a white collar. I reach over and pull a pretzel from behind her ear. Sleight of hand. Afterward, I palm coins for a half hour. A man produces a deck of cards. I do the reverse pass. I do the fifteen-card adding trick. You have to realize that I am not prepared, I have nothing with me. So then I do math tricks—numbers are always good.

The assistant day manager hires me. Only for a half hour, he says. How much could it be for a half hour? I charge him twenty-five dollars—that's how much I thought of what I did. He lives in Massapequa. After I deducted the train fare and the taxi—I forgot to ask to be picked up—I made eight dollars. It is a birthday party. Amy, age nine.

This was what I called myself: *Raemunde the Great.* I owned the right clothes. I basically wear them every day—long black skirt, blue blouse, gold earrings. What I add—you had to add something—is a bandanna. I bought a bandanna at Woolworth's. I couldn't find one that was one hundred percent cotton. Mine is only forty percent. Then I sewed a random pattern of shining silver stars on the scarf. They came in a little cellophane package. This scarf I tie around my hair—pull the cloth down over the forehead. What I don't do is play with the children. I don't say this is a game or anything stupid like that. I am rather solemn. They pay attention. I have no smiles, no giggles. But I hold them, I catch them, they are mine. Wow! Wait until you see this!

I put up a notice on the bulletin board at the front of the bookstore. Also, I put up a notice on the A&P bulletin board near my apartment. "Children's parties," I write. "Economical entertainment." I am willing to do adult shows—clubs. But mostly I prefer children's parties. I like the way children respond to magic. They inspire me.

I begin to be noticed. Good with children, someone says. I am guaranteed to keep them quiet. Suddenly, I keep a notebook listing dates and places. One month I had six parties. What happens?—I am recommended. Word of mouth. I have this book called *Household Accounts*. I inherited it from Grandmother Minnie. I hadn't seen any reason to buy a new one. Some people have to start every new endeavor with *new* things. I wasn't like that. I only turn the page. I calculated. I used a sliding scale of fees. I bought a book with my employee discount called *Knowing New York's Neighborhoods*. It covers the city and an area reachable within two hours from the city. I use it to determine my sliding scale of fees. The first time I charge three hundred dollars—I almost puked. They paid. At the end of six months, according to *Household Accounts,* I could afford to quit one job. Prudence dictated that it should not be Harter's Lumber—but I had been calling in sick fairly often to do parties. My fellow workers were now essentially not speaking to me. How often can flu recur? I gave notice at Harter's Lumber. They gave me a small going-away party—muffins and coffee and a bottle of anonymous cologne.

This is the beginning of what I know is close to "a plan." Then—because life pays you back—I get the flu. Housebound in Minnie's apartment, the water pipes banging with neither rhythm nor consistency, the heat coming in gasps, I wrap myself in a quilt and practice new tricks. I develop my own variations of the egg in the bag. Children are fond of seeing things disappear and reappear.

One afternoon, on my way to recovery, I sit down with a bowl of tomato rice soup and the *Household Accounts*. That is a large ledger—the two preceding books filled with Minnie's bold handwriting are still in the buffet. With only mild and idle interest I take out one of the old books. Each book holds about ten years' worth of whatever she saw fit to put down. Thus, I flip through the sea-green pages. I know whenever I appear: "R. Upkeep."

I am about to have a revelation, my nose awash in mucus, my voice a hoarse croak, my hair uncombed. I turn those pages backward. I am almost at the beginning of this particular book. I would have been age fourteen. The entry is quite readable. "Wired two hundred fifty dollars to L.A., Nat Howell." Sometimes names change. Not to worry, I had been told. They change back. She *knew* where he was! The pipes cough. I pick up one of Minnie Howard's dining-room chairs, with its nailhead-studded red velvet seat, and smack it against the radiator. I hit and hit until someone bangs back.

I begin looking at apartments. I read the advertisements. I have plenty of time. What do I need? I set four rooms as a minimum. I drop that to three and then to two and a half. I look at windows that look out on walls, ceilings that could be touched and not even standing on tiptoe. Real-estate agents don't especially like me. To my requirements, they say, You're kidding?

Owner-shown is better. Some were renting furnished—people going away, transferred temporarily, sabbaticals. Would I take care of plants? Could I be trusted not to rip pages from books? What kind of a housekeeper was I? "I never wax the furniture," a woman warned me. "Or the floors. Ever."

I had been premature to quit Harter's. Children's parties, I realize too late, respond to the seasons. Spring, summer—a bit of fall. Winter is not a success. Parents who hire entertainers are not keen on having a bunch of kids tramp through their living rooms—smearing frosting into the crevices of Barcelona chairs meant to be left as heirlooms. No, winter birthdays went elsewhere, to skating rinks or kiddie theaters.

What else has happened? Carrie has moved in with someone from the Fashion Institute. Lila is living with a man in Brooklyn. I don't think it's permanent, Lila says. But I close off the back of Minnie's apartment and essentially move into the living room.

The bookings begin again in April. I have cards made up in silver glitter on parchment-colored pasteboard—*Raemunde the Great.* My calendar fills. Two husbands call me for dates. One starts off by breathing on the telephone. When I giggle, he identifies himself. A joke, he says. Let's go out, he says. Let's rub together—show me real magic. These contretemps must be ignored.

I have a date with the bartender from a children-adult party. We go to a bar with a miniature stage where the undiscovered vie for fame. You could try here, he suggests. They had a gymnast last week. During a lull in the entertainment he tells me how there is always someone in a crowd who comes up with a drink he doesn't know. He knows plenty, but these people—they always remember one they had been served in another country or on a boat. Sometimes, they would try to get him—but hey, he knew most. "Name one," he begs. "Anything." "The Winter Howl," I say. He smiles. "Crème de menthe, vodka, espresso."

10

I told Carrie that we were like in an orphanage. She told me to shut my damn mouth. Maybe I was an orphan, but they, she and Lila, had a mother. They had a picture. Their mother was one of those soft women, not so much fat but with folds of flesh, tucks, envelopes. In this picture, she was staring straight into the camera. Later, it turned out that she was locked up in Neuropsychiatric— that she got up from the floor after sitting *shiva* for her husband, Laurence, dead at age forty-one, and proceeded to stuff pills into her mouth, anything that was in the medicine cabinet.

Carrie was the fiercest of the three of us. But I was the meanest. Those were the roles we took and accepted. Carrie was accident-prone. She broke her leg; she caught colds that threatened to turn into pneumonia; she suffered from fierce headaches. Lila was the prettiest. She had clear white skin and china-doll coloring. Carrie and I had everything that adolescence has to offer— we had acne and dirty thoughts. We hung helplessly from a branch of the family gone wrong.

Lila was the first asked out to the movies. It must have hurt to lose those looks. That happens. Carrie said it was after a love affair that Lila changed. Carrie said that Lila and this man borrowed an apartment. Carrie met him. She warned Lila. He has the body of a married man, she said, careless and too much at ease. Afterward, Lila lay on her bed and cried for four days, then she got up. Changed, Carrie swore. I wasn't there. To that perhaps I can say: Stories of love are always suspect.

11

Once you do fortune-telling, it sticks to you. People are really willing to believe this babble. Tells you what's missing in real life. This so-called gift for the future follows me—through time and place. How? I don't know. Even into my life with Peter. And he certainly has no faith in these futures.

The doorbell rings. It is Saturday morning, a quarter to eleven. The cypress trees grown as a cluster near the door are a comfort in summer, but now they rattle like empty pipes in the wind. I had already planned my morning, and I was prepared for my activities, my pleasant dissipated attire intended for no audience. Gray corduroy slacks, baggy enough to offer double-knees for each leg and a series of imprinted and ever lower buttocks. My lettuce-green sweater, snagged and looped.

Madeleine, who works for us, has reluctantly gone to town to the market. Peter is lost upstairs in his office. But the problem is the front door, which has a large glass arch on the top half. Divided by spokes of wood, the glass itself is frosted with a design that always reminds me of a bone—a saint's relic, perhaps. Any adult standing firmly in front of that door can see through that glass, at least enough to detect movement.

As the doorbell sounds, I am traveling across the hall, walking slowly in order not to spill coffee from my mug that says in bas-relief "Surrender Now!"

Was I seen?

"Yoo-hoo," the voice calls through the glass and wood aperture.

Trapped by the backhand of politeness. I had been seen. No chance that I could duck down and disappear. One moment later and the doorbell could have sung on. It would not have overcome the music coming from Peter's room, the bass most prominent. But I had been seen and must open the door. On the other hand, consider that it is Saturday morning—no one called to inquire whether they might come over. No telepathic soundings. I mourned the morning's losses. By rights, I should be able to walk away. Still, the backhand of politeness gets you every time.

I open the door.

Betsy Percan, professional neighbor, stands there with a woman whom I do not know. Betsy smiles easily, but then she smiles often.

"Rae," she says, "can we come in? Freezing today."

"Sure." I step back, the coffee in the cup starting a low tidal wave in response to the movement. "Yes, of course."

Betsy Percan is the small blonde woman who pushes past, causing the elegant hairs of her fox coat to billow upward. Who is Betsy? Betsy is a second wife, and second wives in this neighborhood have a beeswax glow and the uniform of small blondeness. She lives three roads away on Thoreau in a monster house designed by Big Money. Peter met the Percans at a town meeting—he a retired lawyer, she the young wife. They have been to dinner at my house at least six times in the last year. But I don't think I ever invited them.

Betsy never minds staring, never embarrassed. Now she evaluates my outfit with a languid glance. I become what? A lout. A sluttish Saturday recluse roused from sleep. The other woman—the quieter, nervous woman—pats her hair, pats her collar. She wears a simple black coat. She coughs, a discreet gurgle. But she belongs with Betsy. It is an impression—satin women.

"This is Alice Shelley," Betsy says. "I know you don't know her."

I put out my hand, do my smile. I am surprised that Alice Shelley's hand is both cold and damp. Sweaty hands belong to different kinds of people.

"I have been telling Alice about you. Miz Magic," Betsy says. "She didn't know you lived in the neighborhood—practically our most famous resident."

What could I do? A churlish hostess struggled inside me: Leave! she would have said. "Come sit down," I say and lead them into the living room. One thing I will say about my living room—I'm not too fond of it. Not all that comfortable. Very white. Like a lounge, a waiting room for the real house behind it. Peter says I am wrong; Peter says that our decorator is the best—he has vision.

"Isn't this stunning," Betsy says to her friend. "Rae's husband did it—with help. But"—she smiles at me—"we have actually

come for a favor. You know about that poor woman in town—
the stationer's wife, the suicide? Marridel Mason."

I nod.

Alice Shelley coughs again. Not real. Either a warning cough
or a let's-get-out-of-here cough. She doesn't know Betsy Percan
that well then—nothing stops Betsy.

"Well," Betsy says, "by the way, Alice lives on Brontë. Quite
close to me. And Alice ordered her daughter's wedding invitations from the Masons—the stationer."

I sit there. What do they expect?

"And," Betsy continues.

"Wait," Alice says. "I might just as well do this. I was in that
store picking up my invitations. They arrange for engraving—
very nice work. Mr. Mason had the invitations wrapped up in
brown paper, except for one sample that he was showing me. I
was admiring it when from the ceiling came these drops. One of
those ugly ceilings—like sound barriers with tiny holes. Two,
three drops on the package. I reacted—I am surprised how quickly.
The splatters were red, not deep, but dilute. I ripped the paper
off the invitations. It had soaked through, but only reached the
first two—I flung those across the room. Then, in truth, I fled
with the rest, stuffed them into my purse. I was horrified—actually quite sick. This is Betsy's idea—coming here."

I am puzzled, and I could see that pleased Betsy.

"Dear Rae," Betsy says, "Alice wonders if that was an omen."

"An omen?"

"You know—in the entire store that the dripping should occur there, right on the invitations. Blood from the ceiling. Is it an
omen that the wedding should not happen? I thought you could
help—hence, the favor."

"How in the world could I help?"

"Don't think us daft, and don't be forever so disparaging of
talent—you have a gift. You *see.*"

"I'm a magician, not a fortune-teller."

"We don't want a fortune told, Rae, darling. You know you

have these abilities—everyone knows. Poor Alice is upset. I mean it is her daughter's wedding," Betsy says cheerfully. Betsy licks her lips, already lustrous.

Have you ever tried telling someone that you can't do something when they are convinced that it is only your mean and ungenerous nature that keeps you from helping them? As for this gift—this false illusion—I perform tricks, and that I have never denied. Why should I? Just their devising and execution is a skill. But as for the future, as for knowing the future—a misunderstanding of magic. Making me one with tea-leaf readers and Ouija-board pushers. I have been pursued by voices that yell like an ancient chorus: "Tell me what wins in the fourth." "Where did I drop my ring?" "Can you help?"

"I couldn't possibly know," I say and turn to Alice Shelley, "about your daughter's wedding—one way or the other."

"Of course," Alice says, "I said not to do this. I'm sorry."

"We know it's not an exact science," Betsy says, clearly annoyed. "But try, Rae, please. How could it hurt? Alice, give her an invitation."

The woman, Alice, looks down; she's very pale. For the first time I notice that, unlike Betsy, she wears no makeup. The woman *must* be upset. So I feel pity.

"All right," I say. "I'll try—but I make no promises." This is the voice now of magic—a practiced voice, its highs, its lows, its resonance.

Alice fumbles at the clasp of her purse. "My only daughter," she says. She brought an invitation. "Betsy said that it helps to touch something—something that was there. I don't have any of the blood-splattered ones."

Helps to touch something! Why don't we simply dig up the corpse!

Alice offers the invitation, holding it by the tips of her fingers. I let it stay there, suspended. After a moment she pulls her hand back. Then I reach out.

That's what happens—you can't get away from this. They didn't want logic. They wanted abracadabra. The art of sorcery. What did I hold? One classy invitation on cream-colored paper thick enough to walk on. No hologram of a low-slung devil, no winged seraphim thumbing its nose. The coppery engraving, Gothic scrolls. Nuptials at St. Andrew's.

Gossip in a small town is exactly like gossip in a city. The town is Berdan, located on the Hudson. The river is sluggish in winter. Gossip in Berdan. What I knew about gossip is that it invites conversations between strangers. It does not matter who the principals are, or whether you really knew them.

I had been to the stationer's store. They sold cards. School supplies tidily gathered in one corner. Children were not encouraged. I imagined that Marridel Mason was the plump woman who sat at the desk behind the counter. A woman who sprayed her neck with a faint scent of lavender. She was too old a woman for the Veronica Lake hairstyle—her hair speckled with gray.

The man—and he was the only other person I had ever seen behind the counter—must be the husband. He had an easy, a nonchalant, manner. Wore a good tweed sports coat in winter. Linen in summer. Didn't dress like a shopkeeper. People said he liked to deliver special orders. Devised special orders.

Peter mentions this story, this gossip, to me at dinner one evening. Horrible, he says. Suicide. But Madeleine has the real details. She tells me while she scrubs the oven. I am drinking a cup of coffee. This wasn't our most intimate conversation. That occurred when I gave her two hundred dollars to take care of trouble. Forget it, I said. I believe that she did.

The town story was that Marridel Mason wore a blue silk dress with a wrap-around bodice, a flesh-colored slip and new panty hose (the torn package was found on the bed) when she stepped in the bathtub and slipped down into the warm water. It was thought to be habit that she had clasped around her wrist the small gold Bulova watch. She was fond of that watch—a high school graduation present from her mother, who had died before Marridel married Lewis Mason. The watch, not waterproof, was ruined. Next to the tub, placed neatly side by side, were the dark blue suede pumps that Marridel usually wore with that dress.

Perhaps she took them off because the idea of shoes in the bathtub was too much. On the other hand, she might have contemplated the possibility of slipping in the tub, wobbling on those heels, tripping and breaking her leg. How difficult that would have been then—like a personal tragedy to have planned death and to end up in a tub immobilized by twisted bones. So the shoes were not worn when Marridel lifted the razor in its safety holder purchased from H. T. Hardware. To scrape paint from the edge of a window, she had said. She made a neat V-shaped cut on each wrist with that razor.

Her clothes, Madeleine said, were ruined forever. You had to be crazy to do that.

"Obviously the Mason woman killed herself over her husband. He sleeps around—I heard that," Betsy says. "Then she left no note. That I see not as hostility but as an act of recognition. It adds a nice touch.

"On the other hand, she was supposedly seen with someone. By the railroad—an unidentified commuter lover. That I can't believe—forget her looks. Apocryphal. Desire lurks under the Berdan elms. But I think she found out about hubby. Or more likely she was told, and the public humiliation was too much for her. So she teaches him a lesson. How does that sound? On the other hand, getting dressed is quite nuts. Makes her look insane. I must admit the tale livens up the village.

"You know, I'm really good at this. But come, Rae, are you getting any vibrations from that invitation? We are on pins here."

Was I getting vibrations? Sure. Ah, poor Marridel Mason—no peace for the dead. I could see—took no special gift—that woman sinking down in the bathtub with its endless flow of red. The blue dress floated up like a parachute holding air. The clothes? I understood the clothes. She didn't want to be found naked in the tub with all those strangers staring at her.

I do my standard head shake, stand up, and carry the invitation directly to Alice Shelley.

"No bad omen," I said. "Coincidence."

There is this long pause. I am supposed to ask them to stay for coffee. I am supposed to. They wait in quiet reproach—then Peter comes down the stairs. We are saved, all of us.

"Hey," he says, standing in the doorway, "I didn't know we had visitors."

I think of Peter as always being prepared. He kisses Betsy on the cheek, she shrugs out of her coat, it crumples around her. I hadn't even taken their coats. He shakes hands with Alice Shelley. Expresses his amazement that they have never met.

"Sweetheart," he says to me, "do we have some coffee and Madeleine's muffins?"

Peter takes the coats. I am in the hall when I hear Alice Shelley's whisper. "I never really believed in that stuff—omens," she says.

"I know," Betsy says.

I fuss with the coffee maker, half-smothered by gasps of steam. It is an extraordinary contraption designed to make many different types of coffee. Peter bought it—imported from Italy. Madeleine swears she hates this thing. When she can get away with it, she makes coffee in a plain pot on top of the stove.

I am wondering if I could get away with that, too, when I feel a tap on my shoulder.

"You looked for a moment as if you were mumbling to yourself," Betsy says. "I hope you aren't too annoyed at our showing up this way."

I shake my head, and open the water well. Madeleine pours into here—and the coffee, I think, goes into the pipe on the left. Or was that when you made espresso?

"It's chilly in here. And it's freezing out. Is there a window open?"

"No," I say, spitefully. Madeleine was often hot. My mid-life, she says. The window by the table is usually open, this hidden by the blinds. Madeleine never admits it. But I know. Peter says that in spring he would have someone check the insulation. The kitchen shouldn't be so cold.

"Listen," Betsy says, lowering her voice to conspiratorial tones, "I didn't want to speak in front of Alice, so I said I'd come out here to help. I got a telephone call yesterday."

"Yes?"

"About you, Rae. I was certainly surprised. Why me, I said. Some man was asking questions. Said it was research. I guess for an article or something. What was astonishing"—Betsy with exquisite grace raises herself to sit upon a stool—"was that—this man—asked the most perceptive questions. I assumed right away that it was scandal he was after. But no, his questions were psychologically based. He wanted to know about your manner, your attitude when we were alone—essentially what we spoke about. You, specifically. Well, I said we were hardly ever alone—I don't think we ever are."

I pour water into the well. A medley of drops splashes the counter. I would certainly have to wipe that up before Madeleine got back.

"Then," Betsy says, "he asked about your family—what you say about them."

"Why did you answer?"

"Beg pardon?"

"I gather from this that you spoke to him—gave replies. Why didn't you tell him to stuff it, and hang up?"

Betsy slid down from the chair. "I think I had best leave. I had no idea you would resent my bringing poor Alice here. I wanted to cheer her up. But you—well, I had best leave."

Sometimes, if you're careful, politeness doesn't shoot back at you. You don't say, oh, do stay. Please. You keep your mouth shut.

I press the start button. Good for a machine to run hot water through it once in a while.

12

Whalen Clarke was my first husband. He loved me. He said that and tenderly touched my cheek. We were married on a Friday in Connecticut. I could have had the wedding either way—he was perfectly willing to have what he called a huge shindig. Tents, orchestras—magicians. A white gown purchased from a salon in the city. His troubled, nervous family in attendance. Neither of us had been married before, so perhaps I cheated him.

In a way we eloped, although six people were present at the ceremony. Whalen had his cousin Bob as best man. I asked Bob's wife, Emily, if she would be my matron of honor. She agreed, although we hardly knew each other, and we never did become friends. I had a bouquet, and Carrie caught it.

Whalen was always sensitive to the moods of life. He insisted that we find a new apartment. That everything between us be right. We developed a deeply intimate relationship. We sat for hours and talked, although we both seemed to keep a certain amount of prudent counsel. He was a bridegroom of splendor.

If anything, this is always a tale about the unseemliness of co-incidences and how we make much of them—the missed airplane, the choice of restaurant, the turning down one street instead of another. All those chance meetings and losses, the misplaced book, the delayed trip become significant. We give them weight, consider them fated. We decline our own impetuous natures. Surely a greater force made us go to that party, with its hired entertainer, and there to meet our future. We gloat over our luck in bowing to these forces. That's how I got Whalen.

I suppose if I were to list certain attributes and certain defects I would create from my memories of Whalen an ordinary man. Yet I pick and choose and make of him the special person. I grant that Whalen was more interested in my day—what I did, the evolution of a new trick, an anecdote about a child, a pink dress, and a chocolate ice cream—than I was in his. What he did was a mystery of numbers and deals and I think some concern with the world's minerals.

I realize how much I am revealing—that his interest or his capacity for interest was greater than mine. Perfection carries with it the need—no, the obligation—to care more about the doings of another.

Howard is not in any way an unusual young man. He is a thin man with a slight build and a myopic squint. I was once asked if that was my type. I have no idea. But what redeems Howard is his wit, his sarcasm. He is only twenty-three when we meet, but he knows the way outsiders do that he is forever eliminated from the center of life. Success meant everything to Howard. I suspected, though, that he knew his future. He has this girl named Amy. She is very pretty. Whalen is moderately amused by Howard, but doesn't really like him. Howard and I have become involved in some local programming, a two-bit show run from Connecticut. He is the announcer. He hates being in front of the camera. And now, he would say, for all of you who are young at heart—Raemunde the Great! Da-da-da—da. I have a cape, a card table, a rabbit. I start talking to the kids—I can't see them, but they are there. Out there.

From this show—my going back, once, twice, calls to the studio—Howard and Amy and Whalen and I end up going to the movies. To dinner in the Village. But together, the four of us, we didn't mesh. Howard's jokes, my raucous laughter. We didn't fit.

It is Howard who tells me to find a name. The Great? he says. You must be kidding. Find something else. But, I protest, I have a professional reputation. He laughs and pulls my hair like the cord from a bell.

Raemunde the Great. I become that as if it is always waiting. Whalen says he thinks the name is all right. Then, perhaps because of the wildness or the yearning in my eyes, he says, It's really good—great.

We have been married by that time more than a year. Our life is not rote—I don't remember that we ever gave dinner parties at a certain time, or attended shows, or even that on cue I decked myself out in the uniform of the up-and-coming executive's wife.

Still, it is a life as doomed to be filled with pain and uncertainty as everyone else's.

What shall it be? The three telephone calls destined to alter my life, my career. I am excited, giddy, noticed. Howard knows that I am going away. Away from him and his friendship. The scene is not unexpected. Whalen is in L.A. Imagine, I tell Howard, they want to see me — talk to me. We share a bottle of wine. Inevitable, Howard says, and busses my neck. Absolutely inevitable.

We go back to the apartment I have spoken about before that I share with Whalen. The cream-colored rugs, the white walls, the slow accumulation of items of worth. The bedroom is not large — it holds a bed shaped like a sleigh, a tall chiffonier decorated with gilt flowers and Chinese symbols. I bought this chest at auction, cleaned it up. I thought it a wonderful thing; at its base are two tiny drawers.

"Hell," Howard says, "you deserve success, babe." "You too," I say generously. He laughs. "Not likely," he says. I insist. I shake his shoulders. Have faith, I say. We tumble together so readily, so easily. Was I comforting me — in an exhilaration of high spirits? That evening, Whalen telephones. My day? I long to pour out the truth. To say this and this happened. The selfishness of confession. We made love — Howard and me. It was good, passionate. As good as with Whalen? No, not at all.

What I plan is that it is over. Yet on Saturday afternoon, when Howard calls, he wants to see me. I say no. Then yes. I am mindful of the changeableness, the vagaries of Whalen's schedule. I know, I know.

Whalen comes into that scene, that classical scene aptly labeled as the-husband-finds-out. Have I lost my senses? To be found on the bed, that bed, those rumpled blue sheets. Sweating bodies posed in a mimetic of natural joy. I know that this cannot be forgotten — entered forever into memory. The pressed flowers of the cheat and the cuckold. I do not think there is even an exchange of words. Or a stunned shouting of names. How could I? How could I?

The door closes. "Christ," Howard says, "I never meant . . ."
Of course he meant.
"Leave," I say. "Leave."

The next morning I am out of there. I pack my clothes, fill cartons for shipping. Take what I came with. What else could I do? First marriages can end this way or they can go on for a long time. I try to think why this happened. But I can't.

I have one last meeting with Whalen, at his request. He wants to meet for dinner, but I think lunch is better. We are sitting in a restaurant. I had never been there before, but the waiter knows Whalen.

"Listen, Rae," Whalen says, "don't leave the city. That isn't necessary."

"I want to," I say.

"Rae—let's put this behind us. Let's do that. We love each other—you are my wife."

My surprise, you can understand.

"You can forgive me?" I say. "How can you? Impossible to forget this—you saw us. You couldn't forget this."

"In time, I could," he says.

I look at him—the very handsomest man in that dining room. I could see three women eyeing him and wondering why he was with me. Maybe I am his sister, they think. They are wrong—I am his ex-wife.

G. I. Rosencantz
Sunshine Publishing Co.
Oleana, Fla. 33546–1075

Dear Rosencantz:

I want to know when you are running my story—"The True Life of Miz Magic." (Regard this as a little hint, Rosencantz—you are not the only fish in the sea.) Also, the title doesn't appeal to me—it lacks punch. How about either "Miz Magic: Her Secrets Can Now Be Told" or "The Fortune-Teller's Fate." Still, I am open to other suggestions.

I haven't heard from you since I sent my manuscript. Why? Surely, it can't be true that you are worried about Raemunde Howard. What I said is the truth—it is what happened. So fear not. I myself do not fear Raemunde Howard. Or anything she can do. And I would tell her so to her face. As a matter of fact—I will. See cc. citation.

Yours,
Carrie Howard

cc. Raemunde Howard

13

Vera calls me. She handles my publicity. Mad Fan strikes again! Don't be funny, Rae, she says. I want you to come in and talk to me. If this person, this cretin, is planning something—an exposé, for instance—well, preparation is everything.

I am practicing right now the Persian version of cups and balls. The Rezvani approach. I'm really good at this. One Saturday I took fifty dollars off a joker trying the Three Shell Game on a card table on the sidewalk. I was out with Carrie and Lila. Know what we looked like? Three suburban ladies standing there with our shopping bags and our good purses. The ultimate gettable yo-yos. After I took that man, surrounded by an admiring little group, we fled across the street into Saks. You'll get us stabbed, Carrie says. We were giggling so hard it hurt. I bet that happened three, four years ago.

The Mad Fan, indeed. Out for gossip are they? Of course, gossip. Listen, I was raised on gossip. Everything, Smyrna used to say, is hanky-panky. Don't believe otherwise. There's gossip in the city, there's gossip among the tribe of Miz Magic—God knows, there's plenty of gossip in Berdan.

14

"I can't believe," Peter says, irritable because he had trouble falling asleep, had not closed his eyes until past four, and now has to face the day, "I can't believe that you intend to be so obvious as to inflict Lila upon Morris Gerry."

"I thought he needed a partner," I say, buttoning my blouse. What I thought was that Lila would like Morris Gerry. I could imagine my cousin and Morris Gerry sitting side by side at the table, analyzing the world, analyzing me, eating a ragout of veal.

"A partner? If Morris Gerry, in the current emotional climate of the world, needs a partner, I am certain that he will ask if he can bring one. I doubt if he has trouble locating a woman."

I thought Morris Gerry was a psychiatrist when I first met him, but he was a radiologist.

"And," Peter says, as he pulls on a gray sweater, "let's not please turn a simple dinner party into a version of Noah's Ark with mating calls. There is no reason why we need an even number of people at the table. Morris Gerry is divorced. Your Lila is not."

"Separated," I say.

"For the hundredth time, so it is meaningless."

We are dressing. Usually we do not dress in the morning at the same time. Also, it is Monday, and on Mondays I sleep through the morning. Peter would notice this change in routine except that he slept so badly. His children are elsewhere in the house. They arrived with an explosion of suitcases. At midnight, he thought he heard those children scurrying down the hall. Once, at two A.M., he considered taking a sleeping pill. He has a bottle of Nembutal, an old prescription. He discovered that such pills have a shelf life of forever. But several years ago he found out that I didn't take sleeping pills. That I never did. Since that time, with discomfort, he too has abstained. Although he had never taken more than one or two a month, now he takes none.

Feeling the unfair strains of that almost sleepless night, Peter neither notices nor comments on the fact that I am dressing. Because I know something that Peter does not, I could have reflected on the possibility that events this day might affect our lives. But I do not.

That is the morning Peter receives the envelope. The envelope doesn't arrive in the mail. It is too early for the regular mail, the envelope is personally delivered, dropped through the slot.

The envelope is thick and rich, the pale lavender intrigues. At another time I could have telephoned Carrie and Lila and told them.

The envelope is lavender, I would say.

Carrie would have howled, her deep laugh echoed onward. Does it come complete with a garter? she says.

Lila would go solemn before saying, Why do you take it?

It's a flirtation, I say.

Carrie says, Such a supposition from you, of all people—life teaches nothing, does it?

But we already know that.

Handling the envelope but not holding it beneath his nose to sniff, lavender scent on lavender paper, Peter says, "From Betsy Percan."

I see that this envelope bears no identifying name on the outside other than the name of the addressee: Peter.

If the envelope indeed came from Betsy Percan, then she must have crept up the path silently on tiny feet encased in the most expensive boots to deposit it into the metal slot. Her car parked at the very edge of the driveway, where its purr would awaken no one.

———

When Peter carefully slits the seal on that envelope; when he shakes out the contents; when he unfolds the scissor-cut bit of newspaper, when he says, "What's this?" I know.

"My God," Peter says, "what in the world?"

He holds up the piece of the *Times,* it catches the breeze from the ventilator, and, if he let go, surely the paper would set sail.

He reads: "Trying to contact Nathaniel Howard last seen 1/10/63 in Chicago. Write Raemunde, Box F613."

"Sometimes," he says, "you are absolutely out of your mind. Why? Did you think no one would notice this?"

"If I thought no one would notice," I say, "I wouldn't have put the notice in the newspaper."

"Don't be a smart-aleck! You never mentioned it—we didn't discuss it." He has never stayed out of my life. He feels no need for that. So he reads everything—my contracts, my publicity— as much as he can. He thinks it reflects the degree of his security.

The notice—the line—is circled with red magic marker. In the margin is printed: "Is this our Rae?" I am overcome by a belated ache of orphanness.

"With a name like Raemunde," Peter says, "who else could it be but you. And why all of a sudden did you want to find him? That man hasn't been in your life since you were a kid."

We are sitting opposite each other in the booth that was there when we bought the house. The ancient red leather upholstery had cracked and has been replaced with red Naugahyde. The real-estate description listed the booth as a charming breakfast nook. But I hate it. Unreasonably, and because I remember eating breakfast in such surroundings when the future did not seem possible. I have been after Peter to have the booth removed. Actually, he has already selected a small table and four chairs for the area. He has discovered that the booth was a nineteen-fifties addition and not part of the original architecture as he had been led to believe. It no longer interests him. The booth isn't that comfortable, anyway. He is only waiting for me to go away for a week or so and he will have the offending leatherette removed.

Is my knowing this magic? I intercepted a letter postponing the delivery of the new furniture.

I lean over and pour coffee. "That ad wasn't spur of the moment," I say. "Second ad. First one was in AFL-CIO state newsletters. I think I covered forty states, maybe forty-three." Cautiously, I butter a slice of toast. I think that four slices of toast with a shower of crumbs are put on a plate each morning by Madeleine to annoy Peter.

Peter only drinks coffee for breakfast. He can bear to look at toast—anything else is too much. His children relish a big breakfast—scrambled eggs, bacon, sausages, tiny sweet rolls dotted with jam. They chew with vigor, make moist, smacking sounds. They eat an hour earlier and afterward Madeleine is ordered to clear the table, stack dishes in the dishwasher, deposit debris in the garbage. The room is then lightly sprayed and the windows opened for ten minutes.

Peter rubs the top of his head. He keeps his hair short, the thickness of the curl makes a part impossible and combing unnecessary. He has been described as a picture-book academic. That amuses him. He is good-looking, but not offensively so. He has the right brow and icy-blue eyes. Childhood illness pocked his cheeks, leaving him with a gaunt and falsely outdoorsy appearance.

I don't know why I put that stupid notice in the newspaper without telling him. True, the replies will go to a box number. And who will reply? No one real.

I slide along the seat to the window. The window has a full batiste curtain pulled tightly closed. I pull it open. The curtain made the day look cloudy, but the sun shines generously.

This is the month when private schools release their charges for a midwinter break. Ours came here; they did not go south. Five or six heavy snows during the winter have left ridges of dirty silver, although most of the snow has melted. The saturated ground means depressions and ruts filled with ice every morning.

The breakfast area faces the part of the property that Peter calls the garden. He had arranged for a small stone patio that is appropriately outlined with plants and flowers, depending on the season.

I like living in Berdan, but I don't feel at home here. In order to see the Hudson, we have to walk down the hill to a wide swath of land that is an historic path that "belongs to the people." We have a survey of this land upstairs in a fireproof filing cabinet.

The noise that the children make sounds peculiarly distant— as they run back and forth, they call to each other. Their complaints are intense. Moving around, probably to keep warm. Even Nathalie seems to forget dignity. They are in the driveway on the opposite side of the house, waiting for rides.

I don't go into New York on Mondays. On Mondays I work at home. Mostly in my office, mostly alone. I don't even have lunch with Peter. He likes to have lunch at the town pub or in a small Italian restaurant that has, he says fondly, terrible pasta. Sometimes he has lunch with a neighbor. But all this is when he is home—like on school break.

"I have to go into the city today," I say.

Peter looks up to see if this is some kind of retaliation for his displeasure. He cannot see that it is.

"Why?"

"I have an appointment with Vera."

At this point I might have told Peter that someone was asking questions about me. But I anticipate a loud disagreement. Safety, security, and privacy will come up and somehow that newspaper notice also. And I don't feel like it. Anyway, Peter has a hard opinion of Vera. So he doesn't ask why.

"Don't forget that we are going to the Percans' for drinks," he says.

"Tell them I'll be late," I say. "I'll come over when I get home."

"By six-thirty?"

"Yes."

It's easy to miss a train. If the train isn't late all by itself.

15

From the second-floor bedroom window, I can look down on the children. They have been outside a long time, waiting. I have a view of the tops of their heads. Ric and Tom, who are dancing wild circles around their sister, have thick hair that defeats combs. Nathalie has long straight brown hair with a distinct part. They all have on the navy-blue coats that they wear to school. Upstairs in their rooms are brightly colored waterproof jackets, but this is only the second day of school break and they need time to adjust. It has occurred to me that my view of the children is often this—the tops of their heads as they wait in the driveway for rides. They are not my children although I have known them for seven years. Nathalie, Sonia's daughter, is fifteen. Sonia's reputation as a painter has grown. She lives in Arizona. She and Peter were married when they were graduate students. Nathalie used to spend August with her mother when Sonia lived in New Hampshire. But now, Sonia says, there are no young people where she lives. It is an artists' colony built on new concepts. They live in a circular house without windows. Sonia sends Peter one hundred dollars a month toward Nathalie's support. She's very scrupulous about that. Sonia's mother took care of Nathalie when she was a baby, but Sonia's mother has remarried and lives in Fort Lauderdale. Nathalie spends the month of June with her grandmother.

Ric is now eight, and Tom, nine. They are the sons of Lutie, whose health, she assures everyone, is perilous. She lives with Andrew, her husband, on Ninety-sixth off Lexington. The boys visit her on school breaks, but do not spend the night. She buys them huge stuffed animals on which they perform operations. Once Madeleine screamed because their bedroom was filled with flying pellets of cotton batting.

The children are in boarding school in Connecticut. They spend July and August with Peter and me on the Cape. Or if I cannot get away, they stay in the house in Berdan. I calculated once—all the children spend the equivalent of three months with Peter and me, eight months at school, and one month with their mothers. Not that I would have it any other way.

Ric sees me watching and looks up and waves. The others see me, too, and they wave.

I know that they have told Peter where they are going. Or Madeleine. Even as I watch, a gray car arrives, beeps, and Nathalie runs down the driveway and gets in. The two boys are still for a moment and then resume their wild running.

My appointment with Vera is at three. Originally I had planned to spend the morning here to work. But that was before Peter received the clipping.

How long does it take before replies reach a box number? None arrived the last time. Who will respond now? This is what I think—ten mysterious letters addressed to Box F613. Eight letters from a Nat. One letter from a widow of a Nat. And one letter from a neighbor of a Nat who is certain, busybody that she is, that the man across the street, the one who looks strange, is surely the Nat—and is there a reward?

My mood is off. There are times when creating is impossible. Peter would have once agreed with me. Creating requires a mood. Now, he would say—a trick is a trick.

What to do until three? I can't stay here. I'll call Lila. It is one of the coincidences of life that Vera and her daughter were referred to Lila. I once spoke to her about my astonishment. Why it should have been Lila from whom they sought professional advice. But Lila only stared at me and said nothing.

Lila doesn't have a secretary. She has a waiting room and buzzes people in and out. She has an answering machine. The private telephone will flash a light. That's the number I dial. I dial right on the half hour. Lila picks up.

"Can you have lunch?"

"Today?" asks Lila.

She knows my habits. It is Monday.

"Yes."

"Something the matter?"

"No."

"Listen, I'm free to speak right now. There's no one in the office." Annoyance appears. "Someone is late."

"Nothing is wrong—can you have lunch?"

"Yes, I can. At twelve-forty until two—or a bit before two. It will have to be around here, though. Do you want to eat?"

"No."

"All right—then that soup restaurant. Look, Rae, I want you to know that I was shown that notice in the *Times*. I can't imagine what you were thinking about. If you wanted to find him—I mean really wanted to find him—there are more discreet ways. I know a number of people who find people—I could have suggested someone. One of them found a father just last week in Hattiesburg, Mississippi. And believe me, this man did not want to be found. The mess he left behind—well, I can't tell you. But Rae, how did you think that people wouldn't know? Raemunde. Just a moment—I have to buzz."

Peter stands in the doorway. Despite his fatigue, despite his annoyance over the newspaper, despite his mild dread, which he decides is the result of the past night, he wants me.

We can lock the door. He could tumble with me on the bed. I am a big, strong woman, and holding me affords him a deep visceral pleasure, he has said. Beyond that of penetration and release.

It is not that he doesn't make love to me. Very regularly, he does. But wanting me, I think, has become more difficult.

I am not insensitive to Peter's misery. I even feel a nice flush. But I am considering what to wear. It is an activity I loathe, this excessive thinking about what to wear.

Um, I mutter, um. Before me, two, three dresses and a shirt are all discarded. If Peter wasn't tired, if he wasn't preoccupied, he would question that. He knows that I do not care about clothes.

"Are you leaving now?"

"What?"

"Now? Are you going now?"

"Oh yes," I say.

There is that hesitation—but neither of us moves.

"I need more coffee," Peter says; the comment is made basically to himself. It is possible that Madeleine will have to make a fresh pot. Perhaps he will stay here for lunch. He will have Madeleine prepare him an omelet. A mushroom omelet. And a salad of radicchio and tiny tomatoes.

Then, if he naps, perhaps he can work.

Winter is easier for me. I can wear clothes in a way that makes me less recognizable. It is children who will know me—sometimes their parents. I am grateful, then, that the day is cold. Another consideration is Lila. Lila has theories about clothes. That certain colors are picked to reflect mood, styles show emotion, overly neat is as bad as too slovenly. It is stressful to dress for a meeting with Lila. I remember grabbing a knit blouse from the top of the hamper, praying that it wasn't noticeably dirty, throwing it on, and being told by Lila, whose eyes did not blink unless she permits, that the green and mauve top reflected my ambivalence towards the lascivious nature of my current life.

But that was a long time ago.

I finally put on a pale blue dress made of lightweight wool, with a tight bodice and a princess-line skirt that flows richly from my hips. Vera selected it for me in January to wear when I received an award from a group called Educators for Children. They gave me a plaque and a check, which I promptly gave to the lady from the Lost Children's Foundation, who was on my left. That woman wore a black dress. In light blue, I televised nicely.

I pull the zipper up, the decision final, when I hear the heavy footsteps. The herd-steps, Peter calls them. I can hear him shout from downstairs. "Stop it! Walk slowly."

I open the door. Ric stands there, puffing, his cheeks berry red from exertion and the cold. It is easier to say certain things to the boys. "Where is your scarf?" I say.

"Don't need it."

"Yes, you do. And take down Tom's, too." I know that what one does not wear, the other does not. "And don't you have ear-muffs or something like that?"

"Oh, come on—we're not going to be outside."

"Really? That's where you have been." I look at my watch. "For over an hour at least."

"Will you call?"

"Call who?"

"Mrs. Straecher. She was supposed to pick us up. Adam said they'd be here by now. Will you call?"

"Yes," I say. I know why Ric didn't ask Peter. Peter would give the woman—the Mrs. Straecher—a piece of his mind about allowing children to wait and wait. Unconscionable, he would say. The woman wouldn't have a chance to say something about the car not starting or anything. And that would be the end of Adam—whoever he was.

Ric smiles. He looks like his father. True, I don't know the mother well. But in appearance Ric is his father's son—except that his skin is smooth. He has a piece of paper in his coat pocket, crumpled rather than folded.

"Here's the number. Give her directions, will you? Maybe she didn't have the right directions."

"Has she been here before?" Was that terrible? Probably I should know if this woman has been here before.

"At school break," Ric says, "last year and this year, too. Or maybe it was a man—no, it was her."

I dial the number. A woman says that Mrs. Straecher was on her way. She might have stopped for gasoline. And she was picking up three, so perhaps this was the last stop.

"She's coming," I say. "Where are you going?"

Ric looks surprised. "To the museum. Natural History."

I wonder if I ought to say that we could go some time. But I remember taking Nathalie to the Museum of Modern Art—long ago, the boys too young. We were on the stairs, going up to the second floor, when two women approached with their little girls.

They wanted my autograph, they wanted to talk about how their children could get tickets. Could they be chosen?

Nathalie grabbed my coat, her eyes blazing with the fever of embarrassment. I want to go home, she had insisted. Nothing could shake her. Afterward, in the car, Nathalie had covered her face. I am mortified, she had said. Mor-ti-fied.

Sometimes it is hard to get past scenes like that. I decide not to suggest a future trip. "Have a good time," I say. "And the scarves—don't forget."

The footsteps descend—then abruptly stop, ascend again. He remembers.

I twirl my hair and pin it up. Dress, high boots, woolen cap, and the loose gray coat. That ought to do it. That is when I pick up the telephone to call for the town taxi.

This is what happens in movies—when the telephone is picked up on the second floor, someone is using it downstairs and the conversation is frightening and revealing. Twice, I found Madeleine on the telephone. Once, she was ordering groceries from the Century Market, although she knew that Peter expected her to go down and select the produce herself—poking at tomatoes, sniffing cantaloupe, and fixing the butcher with the same fierce look she applied to him. No, she was supposed to say, I will not accept veal not properly pounded and as pale as mother's milk. The second time, Madeleine was talking to another woman— perhaps her sister in Albany. The telephone bill that I usually managed to intercept held many calls to Albany. Madeleine's voice had been softer, more girlish and whining in tone during that second call.

No one else on the telephone ever. Peter is speaking. Peter on the telephone. There is another telephone line in the house but it rings only in my office. Peter doesn't like the idea of telephones ringing everywhere.

This is what Peter is saying:

"I've given it a lot of thought. I have read the program. I have to be clear about the dates, you know. Scheduling."

The man says, "I understand. That's why we plan ahead so far. August tenth through the twenty-fourth. We'll be back on the twenty-fourth. Those are firm dates."

Peter says, "Very good, then. I will say yes to doing the cruise. And you'll send me all the details in the mail."

"Absolutely. We will send everything—and there will be an agreement that we shall ask you to sign. Looking forward to meeting you. Good-bye."

Magicians have good reflexes—they practice. Thus, I hang up simultaneously with Peter. Did I hear correctly? But the line was clear. A cruise and the verb "doing." Perhaps that was a mistake. Could it be a surprise? A surprise vacation. That doesn't seem likely. Can't visualize Peter on a cruise. And the dates—fourteen days. Imagine Peter seeing the same people every day for fourteen days. The explanation, I decide, will come later.

Too late now to call the town taxi.

16

At the station I have to park at the far end and walk almost a quarter of a mile to the platform. Made difficult by the fact that my ankles wobble nervously in the boots. The heels are too high. I didn't dress warmly enough, either. I forgot the handsome plaid scarf that matches the lining of the coat and, worse yet, my gloves. I shove my hands into my pockets; the purse hangs from my shoulder and its clasp wedges itself between seam and underarm.

Nothing yet really promises spring. The trees along the Hudson are ash-gray armatures except for one paper napkin that flaps like an impaled wing, its edges caught high on a branch. I see that the Hudson has a glaze of ice. I am walking too close to the low stone fence and move farther away and nearer to the rows of parked cars more fortunately situated than mine. I heard that rats were spotted along the stones, and I think I see a gloss of fur. Big as cats, I heard.

The station is warm. There is a coffee-dispensing machine that also offers fresh-baked muffins. And a newspaper machine. I buy my ticket. A few times I have been here with Peter. He has a nodding acquaintance with many people. Some he knows by name. Many hearty hellos. He has gone to town meetings and on occasion has spoken knowingly about sewers and zoning and paving contracts and whether a new restaurant was the right idea for that empty barn.

I don't feel at home in Berdan. I am fond of living here—I like my house. But I do not feel attached to places. Who can say why?

There is one other person in the waiting room and the woman smiles at me. Carefully, I return the smile. I buy the local newspaper. You shouldn't hide behind a newspaper—I know that. There is always something obvious about hiding. No, simply read. And if you look down steadily, usually nothing happens.

It is a local newspaper. There is no hard news—not even the true tale behind such items as the unfortunate death of the wife of the owner of the stationery shop. Not even that.

What I imagine is a love affair. The stationer's wife and a man. Love, after all, has the power to dislocate and alter.

The train arrives at Grand Central ten minutes late. I cut the time too short. I want to be at the restaurant first. Why? Lila has a series of comments called "Wrong Excuses for Being Late," and that litany will allow her to move swiftly into an analysis of the meaning of my light-blue wool dress.

But sometimes luck is with you—subway trains race in—and I arrive at the restaurant ten minutes early. Well, the place is Lila's choice. An expensive restaurant, if one considers that its luncheon menu consists of soups and salads. A nice room, a city version of a country kitchen. The high cost is probably a fee for time spent at the tiny tables with their white cloths. I will pay the check.

This is the routine. I ask for "Dr. Howard's table." Lila makes reservations. Yes, Dr. Howard has a table. I settle down at Dr. Howard's table. Lila does not approve of drinking at midday. She often says that one should drink only when no further thoughtful activities are required. So I ask the waiter for a glass of white wine.

With my wool cap still pulled securely forward and my light-blue dress minus pearls, I do not look important. Either the waiter knows Dr. Howard or he has deduced that I am not she. He does not hurry to provide the wine. As the restaurant fills up, he forgets.

I turn and look out the window, a narrow view, half-curtained and scrolled with gold paint. How does it happen that I eat lunch with Lila instead of Carrie? Lila would say this is because people change. I think it's circumstances.

Through the window, in among the curlicues of gold, I watch the passage of three girls. One of the girls looks like Nathalie, but it is not Nathalie, because her coat is red.

Perhaps next week I will take Nathalie shopping. I have already written a possible date in my appointment book—for the last two years Nathalie and I have gone shopping on school break. That Nathalie is willing to go with me is a surprise. We spend hours—Nathalie tries on dresses, skirts, sweaters. They drop in expensive layers around her. Does this look good? she asks, feigns boredom, and stands stiffly in something orange. No, I say. Nathalie sighs. She thought so, too, but a friend has the same shade. I pay for these clothes. I don't mind. I have never minded. I am uncertain whether Nathalie's mother has the cash. Sometimes Nathalie and I go for lunch afterward, eating perhaps in the restaurant at Lord & Taylor. I wait for a revelation at these times. I want to know what Nathalie likes most—but I don't ask. Because it would be awkward if Nathalie cannot answer. Still, I am always surprised by the ease of these excursions. Once Carrie says bitterly that the reason is obvious—the girl wants clothes. Simple as that, case closed. Nathalie has more clothes than her friends, but she lends readily.

The three girls who passed all had long dark hair worn in the current fashion—falling straight to the shoulders and parted in the middle. It seems to me that all girls now resemble each other. You must peer closely to pick out yours.

Lila arrives at 12:40. She isn't dressed in an important way; she wears a long and very full denim skirt that adds to her thickness, a too-tight wool jacket, and over all is draped a brilliantly multi-colored woven cape—a river of red to deep purple. The cape was bought in Guatemala and given to her by a grateful patient. I know that story. Lila has rules against such gifts. Here, Lila usually smiles—she is human, and who could resist such a magnificent cape? Not her.

Perhaps the sweep of cape classifies as important, or perhaps the waiter recognizes her. Lila brushes past the staff and heads for our table. Watching Lila walk away is the moment when one of the waiters—not the one assigned to our table—thinks he recognizes me. But he isn't certain.

"Well," Lila says. "You're here."

I am extremely pleased to have arrived first.

Lila drops rather regally into her chair; it is part of her gestalt to permit the cape to drag on the floor. Things have value—but only so much.

"We best order first, though why soup takes so long I never can understand. Have you been told the specials?"

"No," I say.

Lila waves her hand in something like a circle—this is how she also summons taxis. And the waiter arrives to recite the specials.

Lila orders the spring medley soup and dark rye rolls. I ask for a special—the creamed corn soup. And a salad. I want something green.

Lila frowns. "I bet that will come straight from the can," she says, not caring that the waiter is still present. "Cream of corn with a spill of milk. Don't you want to reconsider?"

I shake my head. I was going to remind the waiter about the wine. But now I believe that is impossible.

"Now," Lila says and clasps her hands in front of her on the tablecloth. I think that that is the way she must have sat during her school days, but remember that Lila used to sit on her hands.

She is now convinced that she feared punishment—unnamed punishment. Demons in the paradise of childhood, her analyst told her.

"So," Lila says. "Why are we here?"

"Lunch—for lunch."

"Nonsense—you must have something to say. And let me assure you again that I think putting a public notice in the newspaper was folly. I mean, if you had used initials, but you used your name. Raemunde. Do you know how many people asked me if that was you?"

What I know is that the notice was printed in the tiniest typeface—hardly discernible.

"Six people," Lila says. "If you factor in the number who see it and wouldn't think of mentioning it to me. . . . And re this—if you hadn't called, I suppose I would have—it has sparked something. I received a call about the notice."

"You? Someone telephoned you? About the notice?"

"It wasn't in response to your notice—directly. Do you see the waiter? I have to get out of here when I have to get out of here. But I am certain it was inspired by the notice, considering the timing."

"Who called you?"

"A man."

"Lucky you."

"Oh, stop it. I don't have his name on me. He's doing research for someone who is writing something—he was vague. But not about knowing what to ask. Those were pertinent questions. Anyway, I said nothing. Secrets are my business, you know. But, and I am certain, this inquiry was not benign. You have to remember you're a public figure. Sort of. Anyway, children watch you—that makes you susceptible, I think, and your behavior is under scrutiny. Keep that in mind."

I am suddenly tired. Weary of sharp jabs from the curiosity of others. I still have to see Vera. And if I am not careful, I will arrive home in time to have drinks at Betsy Percan's.

"That call—it's probably because I've announced that I'm

taking a breather, the sabbatical. People ask me what I am going
to do."

Lila does not.

"Miz Magic Takes a Holiday" is what she read in the paper.
Idol of kiddies needs a rest from kiddies.

None of that is true—except for the sabbatical.

"I don't know why you called it that," Lila says. "I suppose it's
because of Peter? Was it his idea?"

"No," I say. "Mine."

Everyone had been angry. Threats dropped. Who does she think
she is? Miz Magic, the two-bit magician. The world is full of such
people. Fingers are snapped—like that she is yesterday. Replaceable. Everyone is replaceable.

Put a curse on them, my secretary suggests. I wish.

Peter is surprised. Actually startled. "I'm taking a year off," I
say. He thinks it over, searches among recent events for a connection. Sniffs the air for other possibilities. Comes up with nothing.

"That," he says finally, "is a good idea. You need the time, Rae.
Your calendar is impossible. I support you wholeheartedly in this."
That was when he put in for his own—he had delayed a sabbatical year from his teaching, from his daily tiring efforts, he said,
until he had a worthy project. Peter and Rae on sabbatical.

I swallow as much of the soup as I can; it clings to the roof of
my mouth. Lila eats everything. She does not have to look at her
watch, she has set the alarm.

Lila signals the waiter for more water. "Know what he asked?"

"Who?"

"Don't be coy—the man on the telephone. He wanted to know
if you had ever, ever heard from Nat—from your father—in all
these years. That, I assumed, would not be dangerous to answer.
So I said no. Then he wanted to know if you ever heard from
that stepmother of yours, and then he went on to everything—
it was astonishing, the closeness of his research."

Possibly the Mad Fan.

"I want to tell you something," I say. I realize that this could perhaps be the reason for having lunch with Lila. The reason that articles in magazines say you don't want to recognize. The unrecognized reason, then. I could hardly tell Peter.

Lila puts down her knife; she was in the process of buttering the last of her three rye rolls. She leans forward.

"Ah," she says, "I knew there was a reason for this lunch. Wait, I told myself. It will come out, the raison d'être."

"I saw Whalen Clarke—two weeks ago."

Lila leans over farther, the edge of the table cuts into her breasts. "Whalen Clarke? I didn't know you were seeing him."

"I am not seeing him, as in seeing him. I mean I saw him. I saw him on the street. He didn't see me."

"Saw him? You mean this is just about seeing him? Oh, for goodness' sakes. I thought it was something sexual. What is so astonishing about seeing—about running into—Whalen Clarke? I'm only surprised that didn't happen before. I'm sure he lives in New York somewhere. I always run into people I used to know. People I haven't seen for years. Roland Draper—remember him? I ran into him at Zabar's two Saturdays ago. So what. People see people again—the paths of life."

"I have never seen him," I say. "Not once. Not all these years. And now I have seen Whalen Clarke three times in the last six months."

"In your neighborhood?"

"In Berdan? Of course not."

"Is he following you?"

I know that I must go on. There is no way that Lila will let this drop. "No, of course not. There's no contact between us. I told you that I just see him—and I do not believe that he has seen me.

"Three times in the last six months. I saw him in Mexico City when I did that show. I saw him in Philadelphia. And I saw him in Vancouver, a month ago." I didn't add how it made me feel. Haunted.

"Are you certain it was him? All those times. I mean if you haven't seen him in years—what is it? Ten years—oh, more than that. He has to have changed, Rae. You saw someone who looks the way he looked then."

"You think I wouldn't know him? I was married to him. Three times—it's weird. Don't you think it's weird?"

"Weird? Not weird. Still, don't mention this to Carrie. She'll think you're deliberately mentioning it to irritate her. Anyway, I think it's coincidence. That's what I say to people when necessary—don't give too much weight to coincidence. Has he changed much? He was very, very handsome."

"He hasn't changed much," I say.

Not as much as Carrie and Lila and Rae.

Carrie believes that Whalen Clarke was once hers. Furthermore, she didn't lose him, rather the relationship was dug out from under her. She fell, she used to say, into a trap of deceit. She was pursuing a career. What career? Never mind. She was seeing Whalen Clarke—and she had trusted those close to her. He could have been hers, life could have been different. The graph of her life could have been different.

That is absurd, I told her. It was a battle, a fierce screaming battle between us that took place in the living room of Minnie Howard's apartment. What was it for her—three, four dates with the man? Carrie is certain that she introduced Whalen to me. She didn't—but she has long convinced herself that was what happened.

17

What do I call them? Sightings. Like of whales. Or rare birds. The sightings of Whalen Clarke. Three times. Is three a significant number? Many people believe that seven is the greatest number of significance. Not me. Chung Ling Soo, the great magician, performed feats with triangular shapes. The use of threes. Unfortunately, he died performing a bullet-catching trick.

My performance in Mexico City, where I first sighted Whalen, caused a lot of problems. They are putting me on film. I depress them. My run-through lacks something. They have a different vision—like the Wizard of Oz. All bright colors. They said that in the rough cut I didn't smile. The children accept that—they are serious, I am serious. The producers believe that my assistant, Max, doesn't appeal to Latin sensibilities. Why, just for them and just this once, won't I use this girl? This lovely girl.

Someone says my gestures are menacing. My hair unfriendly. They want to pin me down—I should do this, I should do that. They couldn't wait to be rid of me. Twice, they lock the door to the editing room.

I am supplied with this guide for tours of the city. Whenever possible, they send me out, and I don't mind.

It is chilly in Mexico City in November. I wear a bulky cotton sweater over my T-shirt. On the last day, the guide dumps me at the airport too early.

We had spent an hour breathing the heady fumes of a herd of cars on the Reforma. I am a disappointment to the guide, a clever and handsome man—he expected more from me. What more? I ate my meals at his favorite restaurants in the Zona Rosa. Hadn't I bought two bracelets guaranteed by his friend to be examples of the highest art of Taxco?

The guide places his restless hand on my knee, presses his silk-covered shoulder to mine. He whispers, *"¿Está usted cómoda?"* But my mood is not good. So the guide—his name is Alfred—is wasting his efforts. I could see his wife. Sloe-eyed, dark hair, docile by nature and training, praying not for his fidelity but only that her husband reappear. What is that? A vision? Not at all. The conclusions of observation.

But, nevertheless, I am at the *aeropuerto.* Left with hours to spare. The long terminal carries the sweet essence of the culture. Cultures have these definitive odors. I have only a canvas bag, which I sling over my shoulder—the luggage has been sent over by the hotel. If you didn't take good care of Miz Magic, she'd put a spell on you.

I buy a package of M&M's, a paperback book with a cover that promises a trillion thrills a page. I consider myself safely in the disguise of everyday life. Most important, my hair is twisted in a knot and pinned up. A disguise. But no, that child has seen me. The walk perhaps. A distinctive gait.

The child shrieks. "Miz Magic!" The voice is high-pitched, excited. "Miz Magic!"

Someone. A mother. *"No,"* she says, *"no, estás equivocado."*

"Miz Magic! Miz Magic! *¿A dónde va usted?"*

Am I truly surprised to hear a voice? That is what is good about performing for children. They see you, notice you, put you into memory storage.

The airport stretches in front of me, a long road. I would outwalk the child. I am careful, keep the same stride, don't look back. Never acknowledge that the lament is for me. I couldn't do that, you see—not with two hours ahead of me, trapped in an airport.

It is safer to go swiftly through the departing formalities and security, and then pick a gate, join a group, hunker down.

At many gates, groups of people wait for a flight. In the months since I have been on tour, I have begun to classify people. Airport people. Something to do. For instance, the silents and the noisies. All those silent single people, or even couples, who would sit quietly for hours with neither book nor newspaper. Surely, fearsome errands are ahead. I say they are not tourists. Tourists are peacock-colored and nervously noisy. They fiddle with pens, writing postcards that arrive home after they do. Tourists can be fat. An abundance of fat people, sweating women, tight-shirted men. Amid a pandemonium of carry-on baggage.

I am not a good traveler. I am packaged—I am a business.

Gate Eleven was a random choice. People sit in the waiting lounge. Passengers for the 2:35 flight to San Diego. I sit in the second to last row, near the wall, open my book. Turn the page, bend back the cover. I sit on that uncomfortable black, plastic-covered, bolted seat.

You know that there are no seasons in an airport, no full moon, no outside. Business travelers unite. I observe this in every airport. Men in suits, never thought to be tourists. Men disinterested in their surroundings. The discomfort of the seats, for instance. They sit or stand and chat about reservations; they sell or manage or survey. They travel all the time. Laugh and slap backs and greet each other with instant warmth. I expected to see you before this, they say. How goes it?

I think I hear another voice. Another child? A shouting of Miz Magic, Miz Magic. I move and am half-hidden by a row of telephones.

The magician notices. In case asked to tell a fortune, I know which lady has the handkerchief with the embroidered initial *A,* which man carries the trace of tobacco smoke on his coat. Be convincing—then you can even levitate in front of the eyes of the viewer. Think of the famous performances of Ching Lau Lauro in the nineteenth century. Or *The Lives of the Conjurers* by Thomas Frost, written in 1876, in which the levitation of a Brahman is described. That man, it was said, truly seemed to float—due, it was believed, to a supreme effort of respiration. Unfortunately, he died without revealing the details.

A group of four men clusters in a half circle near the door that would eventually lead to the plane. One woman joins them. Perhaps the general silence sent their voices onward. All are carefully groomed and dressed. Do they know each other? They greet one another, the nod, the wave. No names exchanged. A conversation about cities, about who has been to Rio and when last to London. They half turn to enlarge their circle, to embrace three more arrivals.

And one is Whalen Clarke, the man in the ice-gray wool suit with the fine white stripe.

I never have those thoughts that begin: Billions of people in the world and then amazingly we meet. Who could have believed it!

Such surprises exist. The indiscretion sighted behind the wall in the darkest corner in the smallest town. Seen by the passing car. Look, look, it's her!

I am perfectly aware that I have only to call out his name—he would look up. Whalen, I would say. Recognize me? He would come closer. Yes, he would recognize me. Well, for goodness' sakes, one of us says. Is that you? Yes, really you. How are you? Where are you? Such a long time.

Miz Magic sits there certain that her voice would tremble, crack, betray her. And why? I mean, who was the injured party? He was.

What did he ever do to me?

This was the first time—first sighting. I believed that I had seen him and would not see him again. Or at the very least another decade would pass. It is reasonable. So I say nothing, wait until I could not be seen, and leave that lounge. Let him board his plane. I certainly intend to board mine.

Therefore, seeing him a second time—and so soon—it is unexpected. It is disturbing. I think immediately of Freud and various cases like that of O.

The second sighting takes place in Philadelphia.

I have rented a car. I am on my way to a dinner. Suburban dinner given by my sponsors, Dimity Toys. Someone would have picked me up. Mr. and Mrs. Daniel Dimity. But with the car, my own car, I can leave at any time. If necessary I can offer the excuse of fatigue. I am very good at this—the fatigue that comes on you suddenly. First, you go into the bathroom and bite off your lipstick, then you powder your cheeks. Emit sighs, design a sterile cough. I can always mention the show, the early hour. *Miz Magic in Philadelphia.* After all, they're sponsors.

I am in this car, this rented car. The heater intoxicates the air with a deodorant spray—spearmint, perhaps. My foot varies the pressure on the brake pedal. The car bounces and a forgotten candy wrapper—crumpled brown M&M's bag—slides forward.

Then the man crosses the street in front of the car, not looking at the driver. I tell you right off the bat that any woman would turn to stare after Whalen Clarke. We all know that certain men do not appear to age as you and I do—they possess the gift of perennial boyish charm.

Whalen Clarke is a tall man, whose broad forehead is over-powered by the serene evenness of his features; his age, of course, could not be guessed. A handsome man, with pale, yellow-white hair and skin a modestly tanned trophy to proclaim that he is accustomed to the sun, but surely no vacationer. His arms swing rhythmically, and in one hand he carries a burgundy leather briefcase with a gold-colored clasp. His suit is a sooty gray, collar turned up against the wind, and no overcoat. Perhaps the walk is short, no more than from hotel to building or from building to building.

By rights, the coincidence should have turned it into a dinner-table anecdote. Guess who I saw in the City of Brotherly Love? A haunt from my past. The ex-husband. I didn't know you were married before, someone might say. There is usually someone to say things like that.

I say nothing. I am not concerned with the smallness of the world. I don't need the other kind of person who nods before suggesting that nothing is coincidence—that life has a plan, if only we understood the quintessence of it.

I am in Vancouver. It is spring. I am with a group from the studio, some city officials. We are leaving Umberto's Fish House. Everyone feels good, benevolent. We have feasted on a wonder-fully extravagant dinner of Dungeness crab. The woman who walks next to me is named Marisa. We laugh, the six of us, laugh and speak about a conversation overheard at a nearby table.

Halfway to the sidewalk—we have crossed in the middle of the block and now wait for traffic—a taxi stops at the opposite curb. What can I say? Should I admit that I knew the taxi would be there on this cool, soft-scented night? Aren't taxis every-where? A man gets out of the taxi carrying—what?—probably a bottle of wine. If I tell you that I believed it was a red Burgundy from Alsace—ignore that.

Whalen Clarke wears a dark gray jacket—one of those gar-ments with little golden sailor buttons—bottle-shaped paper bag under his arm. He enters the lobby of an apartment building.

Watching this, I miss a cue. The woman, Marisa, says, "Don't you think so?" I turn to her. "Oh yes," I reply. I think that may have been the wrong answer.

That evening in my hotel with its wondrous view of the bay, I finish my own bottle of wine. I pick up the telephone receiver. Information has no listing for a Whalen Clarke.

Whalen Clarke inspires anger. Probably just in me. I see him and I am upset, disturbed—angry.

I can remember when he sat across from me at a table in a restaurant called Get's. The restaurant is gone—devoured by the city. Now when I drive down that street I think that the store that sells leather coats is the site of Get's, or maybe the cutesy diner with orange flamingos. I am uncertain.

Wasn't it at Get's, where Whalen said: "How could you?" Oh no, Whalen never says that. Whalen sits there, so cool. Cool, cool Whalen. He never once says that to me. Never once.

So who did nothing to no one?

18

"When I saw Whalen Clarke," I say, "I was angry at him. Really— I was angry. That surprised me."

"Such anger isn't uncommon," Lila says, narrowing her eyes. "Perhaps it reflects on your current marriage—perhaps unhappy. Those kids must be a burden."

"I'm happy," I say. "No, it was anger. And I have no reason— no justification—for anger."

Lila smiles. The ending of that marriage has never puzzled her. She does not believe in the efficacy of the mismatched.

Her watch chimes.

I raise my hand for the check. The waiter either notices or perhaps sees the frown on Dr. Howard's face. She must leave.

"I'll take the check," I say.

"Not necessary," Lila says. "We can split." She looks at my plate.

"I told you not to take that horrible special, but you wouldn't listen."

I shake my head, take possession of the check. That is the end of that.

"This man who called," Lila says. "He was extremely interested in your marriages—knew details. So if there's scandal anywhere, be careful."

"No scandal," I say. I still have to see Vera. And Vera will handle matters. "By the way, have you ever heard the expression 'do a cruise'?"

"Do a cruise? You mean like do lunch? No, I never. No, wait—yes, I have. A woman—I can't recall her name—once said that. She had been hired. Yes, that was it. She was hired to do some kind of a demonstration on a cruise—knitting, perhaps. She said that she was going to do a cruise. No one asked you, did they? I should think that would be beneath you these days."

"No one asked me," I say.

"Wish the waiter would hurry. Tell me, what are Peter's plans for next year?"

Peter's sabbatical.

"He's going to write a book," I say. "Scholarly."

What will I do on my sabbatical? No one asks.

19

I think Nathaniel Howard is dead. Or he doesn't want to be found. That's what I think. People sent me letters. Don't think people didn't send me letters. Strange letters—a few sad, two angry, five requests for funds, one offer to save me.

But Nathaniel Howard is dead.

Leo Littweiler wanted to take me out for my twenty-fifth birthday. He thought that I would be alone. This is before he got back together with that girl, Molly. But I have a lover, a young actor named Walter, who hoped to, expected to, and would use me to help achieve his plans. For my birthday, Dora, my secretary, held a party for me and my crew. Powell, my boss, sends over a large basket of flowers that is heavy on his corporate symbol—the bird of paradise.

A large paper banner proclaimed, Happy Birthday Miz Magic! That is the way Dora behaves. She is sentimental. She is a friend. Dora married three times, twice in chapels in Reno, with canned music, selections from Broadway shows, and rice-shaped confetti, and once in a storefront church—House of the Seven Temptations. She divorced that man before she found out what the seven were. I was certain that no divorce was needed—the lawyer took her.

To Dora, I am Miz Magic. She would have liked glamour, would have admired it, felt it was my due. She only knows me as Miz Magic. She worked for people when they were important, she was transferred when they weren't.

I am always pleased to be Miz Magic. I have no problem with that. How can it conflict with who I am? That is who I am. What I have always been. A magician, a trickster. A magician to children. Easy? Not at all. Children see everything and forgive you nothing.

People misunderstand what a true magician is. They confuse those skills with the role of seance-holders, oracles, fortune-tellers. You can *learn* to be a magician.

20

Morris Gerry catches me in the kitchen. "I called that number you gave me," he says. "Your sister."

"Cousin."

"Yes. Well, I think we have a lot in common. Yes, I think it's going to work out. She's very accomplished. Normally, I find these situations awkward. I suppose it's because she's a family thera-pist—the sensitivity."

"Are you going out with her?"

"Yes."

After dessert—the crème brûlée was declared superb—people get up from the table, the stirring of people. Stuart Percan, Betsy's husband, approaches me.

"I got the damnedest telephone call," he says softly, because he does not want others to hear.

"Yes?" I say.

"About you, my dear. This man calls. Anyway, he actually asks questions. Imagine that. My opinion of you and what you speak to me about—a pack of questions. Well, I said, none of your business. Betsy said it was because of that item in the newspaper. They come out of the woodwork. Anyway, I wanted to tell you. Don't know how they got my name." He squeezes my hand. "Don't worry," he says kindly, "I said nothing."

Stuart Percan is a nice man. He is a nice man with sad eyes. He is quieter these days. Or was he always? What I am thinking suddenly—and I don't know why—is about a tree near the river. Not one of your classical leafy bowers, but something with a prickle to it. The color a dark green, a conifer perhaps—pine, spruce. Behind the station and to the north. I think that Stuart Percan and the late Marridel Mason were lovers there. The ground is hard, stony, chunks of glass, amber to white. Artifacts of last week's civilization. He spreads a blanket, plaid. I don't think they parted. I think she could not bear the pain of what she had done. Meaning no harm.

21

I cannot believe what I am doing. I am following Whalen Clarke. I found out where he lives. Quite easy. His telephone is listed. I believe that he must be on his way home. Not once has he spotted me. I have become a stalker, a peeper, a spy. Think about it—you don't expect to be followed. Who does? This is not footsteps on a lonely street. Daylight in the city. Whalen leaves the subway at Union Square; people surround him. I do not. He lives on Eighteenth Street. He begins to walk. Clouds overhead.

Someone anticipates, hawks cheap plastic umbrellas with green handles.

Hard to believe that Whalen Clarke is in front of me. He is so handsome. Even now, clearly tired from his efforts. A day, I know, that was filled with activities and travel from building to building. He ate lunch in the Hilton with a gentleman who whispered to him. He got into taxis, got out of taxis. I leapt into one. Follow that cab, I say. You're kidding, lady, the driver says.

Do I want to find out about Whalen Clarke? I don't know.

A woman puts out her leg, almost trips me. I know you, she says. Don't I know you?

I dodge past.

She makes a commotion. That's her, she yells.

22

The only people who would understand my new obsession—perverted interest—are my cousins Carrie and Lila. Lila would want me to go directly into therapy. What do ladies want with ex-husbands? she would say. In my experience, she would add, these replayed relationships are all unrewarding.

Carrie would snort. You couldn't keep him—forget your fairy tales. And you didn't want anyone else to have him.

So, you see, there is no one I can tell. I certainly can't tell my husband. Can I say to Peter, hey, by the way, I am following Whalen Clarke—you know, the man I once married. At this point, I should remember to turn around, and often. Can't you just see the newspaper? "Miz Magic Heads for Liaison — Kiddie Idol Goes for It!"

"Hey," Whalen says, "I can't believe it, is that you? Is that really you, Rae? My God, after all these years."

"Whalen," I say, trying not to blunder. "I was just on my way to—" To where? "To see my cousin."

"Carrie?"

"Lila."

We are both hearty, fulsomely loud, our voices a glass of cheerfulness.

"I'm astonished," Whalen says, "I never expected to see you. I figured we could live ten blocks apart and never meet—that's the way cities are. I never married again. Never. You look wonderful, you look great, Rae. See you on television. You won't believe it, but I always tell people—she was my wife. Yes, really, my wife. Miz Magic."

But this doesn't happen. Whalen doesn't turn around. I don't speak to him—that's the way cities are.

Why do I follow Whalen Clarke?

Maybe I hate him.

23

Think about these scenes that I have shown from my life. A slight altercation with my husband, lunch with my cousin, an episode with an annoying neighbor. Hardly secrets. All could exist in your lives. Anyone's life. I do not believe that the material here can be twisted, if the truth is maintained.

I telephone Vera. "I know who my spook is," I say.

"You know? Is it that crazed cousin? It is her, isn't it?"

"Forget Carrie. Not her. I'll handle this now."

"Rae, that isn't wise. Something could happen. I understand these things. Something could happen. Let me."

"No."

Peter is working in his office. I don't know how he can work with the music that loud. But different habits exist.

"What?" he says, surprised to see me.

I knocked, I pounded. But he didn't hear me.

"Turn it down," I say. "Turn down the sound."

"What? All right."

I look at him. I know him very well. For seven years. Now he seems as if pulled up from a reverie, a yellow legal pad on his lap, Mont Blanc pen in his hand.

"What does it mean," I say, "do a cruise?"

He flushes, rubs his head, blinks.

"Oh," he says. "Someone told you. I was going to—but there was plenty of time."

"For what?"

"The cruise isn't until summer."

You can see he is not at ease. Peter is always at ease. But I have come upon him suddenly. I have given him no time. Forget the plenty of time.

"All right," he says. "Perhaps it is stupid. I don't know. They wanted to hire me."

"Hire you? For what?"

"A series of talks—lectures to be given on the cruise. Six. Because of my interests, what I teach—cultural sociology. There is a market for that, apparently. Anyway, I was contacted."

I hold my breath. He was going into the entertainment business.

"What are you going to talk about?"

"Marriage—specifically, marriages to famous women."

It *was* him.

"How could you do that?"

"It's not so terrible. All right, it's not all that dignified. But the money is good. I thought it might be amusing. Then later—I was going to tell you. Well, you have the year off. You'd come."

"I'd come?"

"Well, I couldn't stand being on that boat for two weeks alone— I'd go crazy. We'd have a sort of vacation."

"What marriages? Whose?"

He understands.

"My God," he says, "not ours. I admit I might have been considered because I am your husband. But I made that clear. I'm doing, for instance, Marilyn Monroe, a few tennis stars, a senator—it's all still in preparation."

"Are you asking questions about me?"

"What?"

"No," I say. "You're not, are you?"

"What is this?"

"Nothing."

"Rae," he says. "I know sometimes things between us are not always right. Is this one of those times? Are the kids here too much?"

"No," I say. "Do the cruise. Plan on me being there. Maybe we can take the kids."

24

I am in the middle of thinking about the wrongness of my suspicion—so much, you see, for second sight, presentiments, tea leaves—when Carrie calls me. I don't want to speak to her. I consider dropping the receiver.

"Rae," she says. "Don't hang up, Rae. They are not going to run my story, I think. They are bastards, those people. But they don't know me. Get me, will they! Rae, keep listening.

"You used to say that dumb thing—a million times I heard you say that dumb thing. About how you could have gone to live in Detroit and one day found yourself performing as a magician at children's parties. I used to hear you say that—I never gave it a moment's thought.

"Detroit. I never thought that city was significant. Don't contradict—I know I was wrong.

"Those people in Florida. They traced something. I don't know what. I don't have the money to pursue this. So I am telling you. Minnie Howard was right, wasn't she? Everyone has a secret. If this is yours, Rae, get it out in the open. Don't let those bastards have it. Screw me, will they!

"This is an advance warning I am giving you, Rae. If anything is there, they will find it out—they have the money. But if you're smart—and you're smart—you'll spill it first. Tell the secret, Rae. Maybe it's about your father. I don't know. They lied to me— you're writing the story, they said. And all the time, they had someone else out there in the field."

PART III

◆

On the tenth of June, two days before I became a child bride, I beat Porcelana McDair in a game of Scrabble. She was not one of those old women who had a varnished cane from Social Services and a net shopping bag. She was more the kind you pulled away from—one who wore woolen sweaters in July, muttered about the end of the world, reached out with witch's nails spotted with layers of chipped red, and on her head wore a wig as rigid as a helmet. That was Porcelana. Aside from the fact that she was the best Scrabble opponent I had ever had, all her game pieces were intact. It is hell to sit down and be minus an *e* or a *w*. Porcelana lived two buildings away from us, second floor back, one and a half rooms. Where old people live, it smells. The reason Porcelana's rooms didn't smell was that window she kept open winter and summer. Once a pigeon flew in—still some dried doo on a windowsill.

Porcelana claimed to be eighty-two years old. Smyrna had no objections to my going over there. It was old men who bothered her. Watch out for them, she said. Once, when we lived off Eighty-sixth, we saw this old man in our hallway facing us. His thing glowed, matte white against shiny black serge. He was showing it, Smyrna said. I always thought the man was going to piss and we surprised him. But afterward, Smyrna warned me. No old men. I met Porcelana in the library. Actually, I met her after we left the library. It was past two on a Wednesday. I knew she could hear my footsteps; you could tell she was looking into windows, catching my reflection. I caught up. I go this way, I said. I live in 215. That was that.

If you didn't go to school, old people made the best friends. Because you could see them at any time—they hardly ever slept. Porcelana had a married son, God knew where. They didn't get along. Porcelana said she had been a lover of Ronald Coleman when he was starting out, that she had lived in the same trailer park in Florida as Veronica Lake and they used to get drunk together, and that she had been the mistress of a Bavarian prince named Fritsch when he came to New York for two months. Smyrna said in a pig's eye to all the stories—except maybe the drunk part.

In preparation for the game that I won, I looked up words in the dictionary at the library and memorized them—waiting for an opportunity. These were the words: *oleaginous, zwitterion, phalanx, wyvern.*

I won the game with *oleaginous*—a triple-word score. Built around the core of *gin.* Porcelana was mad as hell. Both of us hated to lose. Porcelana wanted another game, but I couldn't stay. It was nine o'clock, and Smyrna would have ants up her pants by now. She had been asleep when I woke up. Like I said, old people were always awake. It was still dark when I got dressed and went over to see Porcelana. We had cups of hot sweetened tea and started our game.

I looked up child brides—the Tikopia, Kamchadals, Long Islanders of Polynesia. Gifts (the ox, the goat), obligations, and duties. Still, there were basically two kinds of marriages. One was the bride who got betrothed at maybe age two or something to a boy age two or younger—then they toddled off with their mums and didn't get together for seventeen years. Sometimes it was a political marriage and they never got together again. The ceremony was for show. The first kind, then, never did *it.* The second kind was when they did.

Everything in life prepares you—that's what I have always said. For instance, the year I turned eleven I got into bed with a man, which sounds like a nastier tale than it was. That man whispered, "It's cruel, cruel, cruel." I was never sure just how he meant that.

Most important, I was already a magician. Conjuring—the true art, the making of magic—came to me when I was very young. I knew all the basics—the rope tricks with clothesline, the seesaw, the magic box, the dropping coin. I learned that behind every trick, every effect was the explanation. And knowing that made me a realist at an early age.

I had the hands, the movements, even the true understanding of the most desirable illusions, which was rare. What I lacked was style—you know, a persona. I hadn't found my gimmick. No one would watch me unless forced. Still, I expected that to change. I expected that eventually I would *know.* A pattern would emerge, mine. The magic carpet unfurled, I would become a bona fide performer. Take a bow!

As for my ability to keep secrets—wait. Anyway, the man who slept with me was significant mainly because he changed the outline of my life. Although what people yearn for is something like "Girl in Hands of Arch Fiend." Smyrna would have grabbed any newspaper, any magazine that promised that. Listen to this, she would have said.

This man—the one I went to bed with—was not old enough to be my grandfather. So forget those dirty-old-man jokes. All of this happened when we lived in Chicago in 1963, when the South Works was the view—the mountain. Everyone around us was in steel, and Smyrna spoke Polish and belonged. She swore, though, that the language was leaving her.

On bad days, Smyrna grabbed my arm and said that she had created me, that without her I would be in a gutter somewhere, or buried in an orphanage, or dead meat. But for this she had to be in a temper. The facts about life I dug up from the bottoms of drawers, from folded letters, official forms. Who I was.

When Smyrna arrived in New York, I was four months old. They passed me from hand to hand, Smyrna said, like they did to *you*—don't forget that. Finally they stuck me in the attic bedroom of the Kamel sisters. The widows. Don't play music, they said. Be quiet. Must you eat so much? Didn't I realize that *they* were in mourning? Mourning? Husbands had dropped dead ten, eleven years ago. Some mourning!

God provided, Smyrna said. The mighty Celia Claire packed her suitcase. Where were you? She left you next door. Take care of the baby for an hour, she said. Then she left a note for Nat.

Smyrna kept that note. It said, "You will understand that it is best." Then poof—Celia Claire was gone.

Smyrna said. Like that. You were four months old, you were a crier, you had diarrhea, you had rashes front and back. Who wanted you? The grandmother—Minnie—passed you around like a sour ball.

I will never say anything against Smyrna. She raised me. She took care of me. I remember the feel of the hem of her dress and her hands buttoning my coat. Stay close, she urged. When I was annoying, she said I must be like my mother. When I grew worse, she yelled that my mother must have been a whore! But these words were said in times of anger. She was a perfectly decent stepmother. And both of us adored Nat. Once when Nat was gone for two weeks, Smyrna said that she grew a hole straight through her heart. Because I was a kid, I used to have dreams that I became a famous magician and bought Smyrna wonderful things. When I told her, she said to save my money. I didn't dislike her. Our relationship hovered somewhere between liking and pain— we had these common experiences. I never once blamed Smyrna for anything that happened later. Listen, you did what you had to do.

We moved often. Even at the time, I suspected that the starvations of my youth would be responsible for success. Not for me a gaggle of props, gifts of children's kits, miniature stages, fawning relatives ready to believe. I had only my wits, what could be stuffed into a small bag for easy transport, and a series of secondhand books and pamphlets to be absorbed and discarded. Thus, one of the rare copies of *Secrets of Solomon's Magic* went into the trash to die hopelessly among rotting peelings. Memory never let go of that book, with its broken spine trailing gray threads of the bookmaker's art. The cover was black, not a page torn. The illustrations (ill. i–xxxiv) were steel engravings of Solomon receiving his secrets from a brooding chorus of demons, oracles, and seraphims—all in beltless robes. I read that book, and in among the sniffles of prayers, the incantations of how to ruin reputations, the discourse on signs in the clouds, were useful tidbits—the refraction of glass or how to lose a coin in a glass of water, the value of friction, and the possibilities of astounding an audience with numbers.

Even before that, Nate Leipzig, the famous magician, was a hero. I hoped that my father had been named after him. Smyrna giggled when I asked. She thought I was a fool. Nat, though, was solemn. Named after Nathaniel Hale, he said.

Soon after that came my great find in a barrel of books—two for a dime. Years past secondhand, those books were the discards of culture. Here, among outdated guides to the Caribbean, *Fishermen Heroes of 1948, Disarmament for Today*—here, I swear, I found an original copy of *The Anatomy of Legerdemain* by Hocus Pocus, Jr., circa 1634. This latter book I kept with me buried beneath underwear and my two blouses until I left Esher's house. I gave it up only when I escaped and fled from my Chicago fate. Give up anything, Nat had always said. I had no choice—the book was heavy and would have been noticed.

It is not my custom to dwell on past phantoms. Not that there aren't effects. Certainly there are effects. What do you expect? Perhaps I should have grasped my own hand and told a fortune. See, see. The Lifeline, the Heart line. The trip and the dark tall man. Nothing that I tell you is intended to change what happened the year I was eleven. Only to explain how we came to be in those circumstances. Explain, you understand—not apologize or correct or offer metaphysical twaddle.

It was on my way home from Porcelana's the day I won at Scrabble that I realized—realized just like that. I was a June bride.

Smyrna was up and vacuuming. "Sit down," she ordered. "What kind of idiot goes out *this* morning!"

"You want me to help?"

Smyrna made a noise—a haruumph. Once Smyrna took a job as a maid in a house off Devon Avenue. When she came home, I must have said something, because she grabbed my shoulders and shook me until my head throbbed. Then she stopped. The next morning she said she'd walk the streets first before she'd go back.

She was not much of a housekeeper, but when she decided to clean, she went at it with frightening intensity. Already the refrigerator stank of bleach. The poor thin carpet was prodded from the gray-tweed suppurating loops to its already cracked, glue-strengthened backing—the Hoover was borrowed from the woman upstairs, the one with the black mole on her lip. Smyrna's voice echoed through the hall with the power of forced neighborliness: "Bring it right back!" Now she shamelessly banged the metal again and again into the legs of Zeidner's second-best, reupholstered-like-new sofa, a chip of varnished wood chopped smartly off one trembling pedestal to be gobbled by the wheeled chip destroyer.

Smyrna normally coated herself with a can of carnation-scent bath powder from Walgreen's and that smell, now mixed with her own odor, sent forth a rich aroma to season the air.

Smyrna was thin except for the breasts. They swung, those weights of flesh, as if loaded by age, as if she'd had children who had milked them dry. She hated to wear a bra, hated the way it pinched and hurt, embarrassed to buy a bigger cup. Whenever she could, she went without. She shoved my chair. It was that unexpected jolt to the nervous system that made me jump. I had been reading, sitting in that chair, legs draped immodestly across the arm. "Move, bookworm!" Smyrna ordered. I stood up, dragged the chair forward, the vacuum pursued it. All the time Smyrna looked at my legs. They were skinny, those legs, covered with a fine down of palest brown. A kid's legs. "What's that?" she said and pointed.

"What's what?"

"That! That!"

"That's a scab—what did you think it was?" The silhouette of the scab was like a rock in pink water.

Smyrna bent over to see the offense more clearly. That raised mountain just above the left knee. "How'd you get that?"

"What do you think? Maybe I got it fishing, huh? I fell. I tripped on the stairs." Was I now damaged goods?

Smyrna shook her head.

"Maybe I should wear stockings—you know, and your black pumps?"

It was foreign territory for both of us.

"No," Smyrna said. "No stockings. God, I better take my shower. Look at the time. Listen, take this thing back upstairs to that woman. Just our luck she'll come looking for it when Theodore is here."

"All right," I said and settled back.

"Now!"

Who were our preparations for? His name was Theodore Wilson Fine. Which tells you right away that his parents were immigrants with pretensions. He was smooth; he was polite. I would have preferred a more macho stance. But he was decent looking. Small and skinny, but decent looking. He stared at me a lot. He wasn't a smiler. Me—I asked a lot of questions. Him—he asked nothing. Just a skim of information—all on the order of how's the weather.

Smyrna didn't hold back. Everything Teddyboy said, she repeated to me. That's because we were uncertain and, in truth, we were all nervous. Except for him. What was going to happen? He wanted to buy me. We could call it by one hundred fifty names— but that was what it was. I never thought he was getting a deal. Say what you will—Theodore was probably a man that women liked. He was pensive in manner. I bet he held doors open.

We moved so often that telling the story of my life changed. Smyrna would say that no one had to know everything. In my last school, I had a friend named Elizabeth. She showed me how to put on a sanitary pad and what the various holes in my body were. She and I were becoming thick. She said that someone liked me and pointed him out. That evening I took off my clothes in the bathroom. My chest had only the faintest rub of flesh, a set of tiny pink nipples. Next to Smyrna I looked like nothing. And standing there by myself, naked, I was surprisingly shy. I used to wonder about Smyrna's body. She was not modest—anyway, she had dark, thick pubic hair, and the hair under her arms was dark and, if possible, thicker. But her arms and legs had hair that was as pale and vague as the white-corn hair she combed. I only had a streak of fuzz—a handful of hairs. That was only three months ago. Had I changed? Theodore was going to be surprised.

Theodore Wilson Fine was a salesman who lived in Detroit. He sold locks, wholesale—locks, special doors, bolts, grills, devices. He was an indoor man, with a pale face the color of blanched nuts. Smyrna and I did that once, years ago. Fixed blanched nuts for a special frosting for a birthday cake. For Nat. Theodore looked exactly like those nuts—original color removed. Except for his eyes. Oh, his eyes were honeys! Movie-star eyes with a curl of coal-black lashes. Smyrna said that life did that—gave lashes long enough to comb to a man who didn't need them.

Soon as I heard the water pound in the shower, I dragged the Hoover upstairs, banging it from step to step. Its owner opened her door wide when she saw it was me. The woman smiled. I couldn't believe that she had ever been pretty. It was impossible to look at anything else but that mole, half of her lower lip hung with that wiggling sac of blackness. "Getting company, Rae?" she said and winked. "Your mom has a boyfriend, no?"

"No," I said pleasantly and turned away. Rats on you, lady.

We met Theodore four weeks ago. We met him at a party at his sister's apartment, where he was staying. Neighborhood parties are part of what Smyrna did. She understood the fine points of acceptance. Anyway, she donated the bread. Everyone was glad to see her; she had the right melody. Big hellos. There was nothing for me. The sister didn't have any kids, so those that came stayed outside. You had to go to school to belong. I left the crowing women and hunted for a bedroom to read. That's where I met Theodore.

I walked into this room and there was this man perched on the edge of the bed, writing in his salesman's notebook and whistling something tuneless. The best whistler I had ever known was

Nat. He could whistle entire songs so that you could actually think a singer was there and the orchestra. Theodore made only the whistle sound, up and down, but no tune. I backed right out. But he heard me. He looked up, frowning. It's all right, he said. He saw the book. If you want to stay and read—stay. So I did. That was the first meeting. Now, I didn't go home and dream about him. I knew girls who would have taken a notebook and written "Mrs. Theodore Wilson Fine" a hundred times.

Chicago was part of Theodore's territory—whenever he was in town he saved money by staying with his sister. The sister was Esher—a genuine pain in the neck. Esher wasn't a special friend of Smyrna's, but they had met in the laundromat. She knew me, too. She didn't like me. You can tell that right away. She stared at me as if I came from the darker side of America. I thought she mouthed the word *trouble* the first time she saw me. Sometimes disliking can be instinctive, hormonal, olfactory. She didn't like me, and I couldn't stand her. If I knew her a thousand years, I wouldn't like her. She had flabby cheeks. Her body, though, was enormous and firm. Look at that, I said the first time I saw her. Smyrna told me to shut up, said my whispers carried.

How we got to this apartment? Our apartment was on the next block. We got here because my father, Nat, had gone over the fence, in a manner of speaking. He had left before, but this time it was different. Sometimes he'd give a quick good-bye, or we'd all move real fast.

This was different. We had lived near the South Works. Smyrna hated it, swore the Calumet River stunk. Whatever Nat told Smyrna, she was still afraid. Maybe she had heard something when I was in school. Anyway, she was sitting by the window when I came home one afternoon—stopped off at the library, so I was late. Smyrna was in a temper, chewing her fingernails. The Chevy station wagon was packed—a mess tumbled in the back.

"Where the hell were you?" But Smyrna didn't wait for an answer. We were gone. I still had that library book.

If I learned anything, it was when to shut up. We had never moved without Nat—no matter what. It was Nat who carried the cartons to the car. Nat who always said calm down and take it easy.

Nat had been gone ten days—ten days on Monday. We lived on Mackinaw, on the South Side. I went to Fred C. Carpenter Elementary. I hoped we'd stay in the district. Somewhere.

Once I asked Smyrna if Nat was a crook. I mean, people knock on our door in the middle of the night, and I know for certain that he kept a gun in his sock drawer. Smyrna giggled. It was genuine, she started holding her sides. "If he were a crook," she said finally, "we'd be rich."

I wondered how Nat would find us. There must be a signal— that was the way it was in movies. Maybe Smyrna had to go to a telephone booth or something. Smyrna didn't say one thing, she drove that car, she cursed the other drivers. But she didn't even tell me not to turn on the radio.

Smyrna registered us at the Bide-a-Nite on I-57. Smyrna thought they'd rob us blind. I looked around and agreed with her. So we hauled in all the stuff from the car. Smyrna said that I would have to stay and guard it while she went for food. I took out my deck of cards. Nat gave them to me—the backs said Illinois Central. I practiced cutting. I did a neat one-handed cut—no one would see that happening. It's called a pass. The deck was poker width— harder than making a pass with bridge-sized cards. Hands were everything. Smyrna was never interested. She wouldn't watch even when I mastered the Reverse Charlier Pass. Charlier was a great magician, cards mostly. One day they'll name a trick after me. My whole name—more pizzazz. The Raemunde.

I turned on the television. You didn't exactly have to kick it, but close. The picture was half snow. The room was lousy—even for us. Smyrna came back with hamburgers, French fries, two Cokes. We watched a cops-and-robbers, then the news. I didn't try bouncing on the bed—it felt collapsible. The bedspread scratched, but I fell asleep on top of it. When I woke up, it must have been the middle of the night. Smyrna had poured herself a drink from Nat's special whiskey bottle. She was reusing the paper cup from her Coke. You'd have to be out of your mind to put anything in the glass the motel supplied. I pushed up my pillow and watched the movie for a while. It was *I'm All Right, Jack.* I was nuts about Peter Sellers.

Bide-a-Nite was the pits. "I can't stand this," Smyrna said. So we piled the stuff back into the car. It was my suggestion that we stop at an A&P and get some boxes. If we were going to haul this stuff in and out, it was crazy to grab three pairs of shoes a trip.

We didn't move to this apartment right away. We did what Nat used to call the tour. I could forget Fred C. Carpenter Elementary. We took furnished rooms for two weeks, then moved on for four weeks, then six. When we stopped for four weeks, Smyrna took a job in a restaurant. Not waitressing. She worked in the kitchen.

I suspected she must have got the idea for me from Nat— Smyrna didn't think of things like that. I was to limp, she said. A little—nothing to call too much attention. The story was I had had an operation, now recovering. Staying out of school for a while. That worked.

What Smyrna always understood was nosiness. Whenever we landed, she would walk the neighborhood—she was shrewd about that. She could sense where to go—sometimes a butcher, sometimes a laundromat. There Smyrna would manage to introduce herself—her new-in-the-neighborhood act, tell some dumb but believable story about us, offer unasked details. Before you could say Jack Robinson, she was one of the girls, if you know what I mean. No one was curious—if they thought you wanted to tell.

The kitchen job gave out when the counterman put his hand up the back of Smyrna's skirt to the spot where her tight cotton briefs hugged her buttocks.

Smyrna turned and raised her knee. Then she grabbed his hair and brought the moaning head down right on the edge of that steel counter. Chipped a tooth. The owner was sympathetic, but the counterman was useful. Smyrna was just a stirrer and cutter. She went.

Smyrna came home. I knew, because it was only four o'clock. She smoked two cigarettes real fast. "Listen," she said to me. "I can do nothing. I know that I can do nothing. Always know how to do something, Rae."

"All right," I said. I already knew magic. But I kept my mouth shut. No point in bringing up a sore spot.

We moved the next day. Smyrna found this place. "A dump," Smyrna sighed. "But we can stay awhile."

This was now home, and better than most. We lived furnished always. But don't think that meant everything—we always had to add to the kitchen, carried spare blankets, an extra lamp. Furnished came in gray and dark green and brown. Furnished also was tweed. You can spit in tweed and never see it. Here, we were lucky. The landlady had bought the building a year ago and changed it from a four-family into an eight. The dream of her life, I figured. The furniture, you see, was new. Or new secondhand, anyway. The walls had no one's smear. Even the toilet seat lacked the stains of iodine. We had three rooms, front corner left. The landlady said a widow and her daughter were fine, hunky-dory. In honor of the newness of the couch and one armchair—four pieces of crochet decorated the backs. For hair grease, the landlady said. Smyrna nodded her agreement, oh, yes sirree, and as soon as the woman toddled off, we took the crocheted hair rags and threw them on the closet floor. People had to take their chances when they rented out furnished.

I knew that we were going to stay here—where we were— for at least three months. First of all, we needed money. Smyrna went out and got part-time at the Elite Bakery, and Saturdays and Sundays in the cafeteria of St. Joseph's Hospital. Me—I was still to limp. In three weeks I could be cured—school would be out.

In less than a week, Smyrna was first-names with all the busybodies and yentas on the street.

———

The bedroom was such a mess that day, you would have thought Smyrna had the wardrobe of a movie star. Brassieres dangling from the pillows, slips wadded into balls. Shoes mixed black with white and blue with brown. Smyrna herself stood sweating in the middle of the room. "What? What?" she declared. Was the choice endless? Blue brocade versus yellow satin? Forget that. She had four dresses, two skirts, four blouses—although one had pale beige stains that could not be scrubbed away.

She had washed—witness the bathroom, the towel dripping on the floor, the razor used to grind a stubble on her legs. Smyrna was never one for neatness, but—by and large—she managed. She sweated as she stood in the middle of the room, fresh talcum powder pounded and pressed onto her back and arms and between her moist thighs.

"Wear the white," I said.

"The white! What am I supposed to be—the bride?"

The sarcasm was natural—but the circumstances were different. Smyrna had spoken too quickly. She flushed, her entire body pinkened under its mask of white chalk. She grabbed a brassiere, hefted it as tightly as possible, until the straps made deep grooves on her shoulders. The look for the day was decorum.

The white dress was really the best choice. Two others were funereal in design—suitable for ceremonies, which this was not. The other remaining choice was a working woman's dress made to be worn with downcast eyes and an air of supplication. No, the white was absolutely right. A cocky, almost showy dress. I was surprised that Smyrna had ever bought it. It must have been Nat's idea.

Smyrna motioned to me, and I came around and zipped the bodice. It was snug and the neckline low. One bend and there was her cleavage. We both stared straight ahead at the mirror and almost simultaneously nodded.

Smyrna started to pick up the clothes. "He isn't coming in here," I said. "Close the door." I looked at my reflection then. "Can I wear the black pumps?" They were Smyrna's, but on two occasions I had been allowed to borrow them along with stockings with a silky feel that I adored.

"Are you crazy?" Smyrna said. Now her attention turned to me. I got the customary rough jerk around. She straightened my collar, wet her finger, and smoothed my eyebrows. I hated that, pulled, but her hand was the stronger. My hair was brushed straight back. Long hair that went at least an inch below my collar. Mud-colored hair, I thought. If it hadn't been for this visit, Smyrna would have let me cut it. It was a mess to wash. But now, everything was being kept the same. Everything got a later as answer. I wore my white school blouse and my navy-blue skirt. White ankle socks and my brown loafers, scuffed at the toes.

"You'll keep still," Smyrna reminded.

I shrugged. "Who wants to talk anyway?"

We were set, as far as I could see. Bring on Theodore!

"What should I offer him?" Smyrna mused.

"Offer him?"

"To drink, stupid—what?"

"It's hot," I said. "Iced tea maybe."

Smyrna nodded. "And I'll make coffee, too, in case he wants that."

The kitchen was small. In the refrigerator was a plate covered with wax paper. Pretty little squares of cake from Smyrna's day job—petit fours. La-de-dah cakes for a wedding reception to be held in the basement of St. Anthony's. Smyrna had lifted them from the edges of a platter, secreted them with effort in the bottom of a bread bag. Somehow they had arrived without damage. I was dying to taste one, but there were only six—it wasn't like I was taking from a whole platter. Theodore didn't strike me as a man of appetite—Smyrna wasn't much for sweets herself. There would be at least one left for me.

"That's it," Smyrna said, "the best I can do. You sit in the chair. Stay neat. Be still."

I gave my special, little-girl, stupid smile—it wasn't a look she liked, but considering the day I knew I would get away with it.

I thought the place looked as good as it could. The room didn't have much—the couch in a color that must have started life as faded green, and the single gray-brown armchair that I had pulled over to the window first day we arrived. The view was only of the street, but when you read, the light from the window was better than the lousy lamps we had. We used to carry two of our own, but Smyrna left in such a hurry that we forgot one of them. She mourned that—two matching brass-plated lamps.

I sat down in the chair. I had a library book. The local one wasn't the world's best—I was debating whether I ought to ask them to get things for me from other libraries. Was that risky? They had the standard magic books. Nearly two thirds I already knew. Still, maybe there were new angles. Stuff I had missed. I started to read. Smyrna sat on the couch. There was nothing more to say.

For a while I couldn't concentrate; I had no experience in these matters. Did I owe Smyrna? I believed that I did. She was always decent to me. And we loved Nat—both of us. Just the week before, we were sitting in the living room, watching Joan Crawford talk a guy's head off, when we heard footsteps in the hall. They were of a certain weight. Smyrna and I both turned. It sounded like Nat. If Smyrna thought Nat was coming back, none of this June-bride stuff would happen. But she didn't. After those footsteps, Smyrna went and poured herself a drink.

These were the terms. Theodore Wilson Fine was going to pay Smyrna the sum of five thousand dollars. Actually, neither Smyrna nor I believed in that money—it was not a sum we could grasp. But Theodore, my Teddyboy, was to give that to Smyrna if we agreed. Like a trade—for me. First, he had established that Smyrna wasn't the mother. Not hard, since we don't look like each other. Nat was definitely the father. Out of the clear blue sky, Smyrna told Theodore that *my* mother had the last name of Cohen. Oh, brother! I mean Celia Claire was all I ever heard. Well, Teddyboy was easily satisfied, I guess. Next, we had these solemn walks— him, me, and Smyrna. And he quotes. From the Bible? Who knew? His favorite was from what he called the *Tosafot*. This interpre-

tation, he said, was very subtle. "The circumstances of exile re-
quire that our daughters be betrothed before they are twelve
years old," says our Theodore. "No, more than required—it even
could be claimed that the situation of exile compels this." Amen.

Yes, he planned to marry me.

I have a lot of respect for coincidences. Pay attention, and a
lot of magic can be learned. For instance, I liked to look over
books that people returned to the library before they were shelved.
That was where I saw this book—the one that I kept under my
bed. Already it was overdue. It was a book of photographs. Now,
photographs didn't mean a thing to me. This was a famous book—
the librarian told me that. What did I want it for? One picture. I
just came upon that picture. Although Robert Houdin believes
that everything is found for a reason, I myself was uncertain.

The black-and-white photograph on page 102 was of a girl
standing on a road by a shack. In a movie, I knew she would be
white trash. In this picture, this girl was standing in a field or by
a dirt road, the shack in the background to the left. She was a
bony girl. She had dark hair about shoulder length—hung straight,
no wind. She wore a plain dress with an itsy-bitsy print—couldn't
make out what it was. The girl stared at the camera and never
smiled. Just stand there, I imagined someone said. Don't move.
Just stand there. Three kids clung to her knees—they grabbed
the dress or her body.

Theodore Wilson Fine was due at eleven. A peculiar time to
plan to come, Smyrna had thought. We had debated whether to
offer lunch, but that seemed impossible. What did he eat? Smyrna
was no great cook. We could bring in prepared. Would he eat it?
Chinese?

I settled the matter. If he asked to come at eleven, and no one
mentioned lunch, then he can't expect any. Let's not. I mean how
much did that man want? Smyrna agreed with relief. No lunch.

When the doorbell rang, Smyrna shot me a look. What had she
thought? I was watching out the window? Actually, I had begun

to read about an illusion with marbles that I had never tried before. I had my doubts. Some people will write down anything. I hadn't seen Theodore arrive. I actually had forgotten about him.

"Coming," Smyrna sang out, in a voice that wouldn't fool anyone as being normal.

I had no idea how old Theodore was. But he was no grandpa—that was clear. Old men could take a flying leap as far as I was concerned. When Theodore stood next to Smyrna—they looked all right. Like they could be going together or be married and no one would give a second glance. And Smyrna, I knew, was twenty-eight. I knew that for a fact because I read her immigration papers—took them from the accordion folder with the knotted string. So that made Theodore somewhere in that neighborhood. No grandpa.

Before we moved here, when I was a registered student at Fred C. Carpenter Elementary, I knew a girl in junior high who was going for the title of Miss Cloakroom of 1963. She hummed love songs, put cologne inside her panties, and in winter she had one of those won't-go-away colds that left a shine of mucus around her nostrils. It was said that she didn't refuse anyone, but only the bigger boys took her on. They came in pairs and one of them would hold her—never mind that she was supposed to be as still as a lump—and another one would do it. A few girls swore they witnessed the act—details were sketchy. A list appeared on the blackboard one day in the weekly class called Health. "What I want in a Man: Big build, tall, black hair, horny arms." The teacher erased it, but first she defined horny.

Theodore reminded me of Tyrone Power, although I wasn't all that crazy about Tyrone Power. But he was close to being a dreamboat. Theodore was not tall—he wasn't more than three inches above me when I wore my loafers. He was skinny, too. And tall was one of my secret requirements. Also, broad shoulders. Theodore had thick black hair—a plus. I couldn't get used to his clothes. Basically, I thought men should wear what Nat wore. Last time I saw Nat he wore mostly flannel shirts and khaki pants or jeans. Once in a while he wore his tweed jacket and gray pants—he wouldn't own a suit. Certainly not one like Theodore wore. Theodore always wore a suit. It could be hot enough to die, and he would have on a suit. Black suit. Natty, Smyrna said. Dumb, I said.

The wheels were turning in Smyrna's head—that I was certain about. How much was she in control? Last time Theodore spoke to her. We had gone for a walk to Jackson Park. Smyrna was going on about the weather and the pretty flowers and what a good student I was. When out of the blue Theodore said, "Does she have her womanhood yet?"

I nearly choked on a red-hot.

Smyrna—and up to now I would have said nothing shocked her—turned a shade of venous blue, skipping pure red altogether. It was the word. Smyrna could have taken the curse or period or her little visitor. Any of that crap.

But with one word—Theodore had gotten her.

Well, she swallowed her saliva and tried to turn smooth. It wouldn't have fooled me.

"Yes," she said, her voice a benign whisper. Then she thought more should be said—maybe pretending she was speaking to a doctor. "Six months ago, actually. They do that young these days."

I think she could have kicked herself for the young part.

Now I really liked the word *womanhood*. I practiced saying it in the bathroom. I paraded past the mirror. I have got my womanhood.

Theodore gave me one small nod when he arrived—like, I know you're alive. Then I figured that he upset Smyrna. She sat down at one end of the couch—I guess she expected him to sit at the other. This wasn't a big couch. But no, easy as can be—he sat down next to her, less than a cushion's breadth away. She sat carefully, hands in her lap—I smelled her across the room. Sweet.

I looked at my book. I tried to figure out if the marbles could be shifted that way from second to third finger—wouldn't one drop? The magician make a public idiot of himself? My fingers moved. My fingers were skilled, deft—if you didn't practice, forget it.

This was the day for final plans. Smyrna said I could back out. She said I could back out anytime. Look, Smyrna could have dumped me. Anytime, she could have dumped me. I wasn't her child, after all. The strangest thing was when it turned out that Smyrna knew someone in California. A friend from Cracow, she said. A woman named Gemulda. I would have, up to that time, sworn that I knew all there was to know about who Smyrna knew. That was what she would use the five thousand dollars for—to go to California. All of this put together made me know that Nat was not coming back. I never thought he was dead. Although Smyrna had a death dream once—woke up yelling. Told me she saw Nat under a pile of old rubble—tires and bricks. She shivered and cradled her arms. I made her a cup of coffee.

We were almost out of money. Smyrna couldn't find a job that paid good wages. One way or another I was going to have to go somewhere. That's why it seemed fair for Smyrna to have the five thousand.

Theodore and Smyrna were going through the plan. I knew the details already. All the quotes from the Tosafot, or whatever, that made it possible, if not legal. Smyrna got up and went into the kitchen. I'll say this for Theodore, he didn't once turn around to look at me while she was gone. She came back with two cups of coffee. Either she forgot the cakes or he didn't want any. Smyrna was sweating again. I saw the shine on her forehead before she sat down and the nervous plucking at that tight bodice—it must be raining under there.

Theodore said that his family followed the teachings of an ancient scholar. They weren't mainstream, they were different. I would have instructions, he said. I could hardly wait. Meanwhile he offered Smyrna the marriage contract—his version, the *ketubah,* he said. According to this document, I was to become Theodore's wife to be sheltered and fed, and Smyrna was to receive a gift of five thousand dollars.

I wished I had my deck of cards with me—my fingers twitched with the urge. I should have hidden them under the seat cushion. Smyrna would have had a fit. He won't know they're for your stupid tricks, she would have said. He'll think God knows what.

Like I said, I got lost when I read—I knew that. Theodore was standing next to me. When I looked up, I realized that he must have been talking, because Smyrna had one of her drop-dead looks aimed at my head.

"What?" I said.

He smiled. "I asked if you would like to take a walk?"

"Sure," I said, put down my book. Then I remembered. We'd practiced. "Is that all right?" I asked Smyrna. I had to keep from laughing. I mean, listen to me—the unchaperoned virgin!

"Yes," Smyrna said, catching the cue. "Certainly."

Then we left—Theodore and me. He held the door for me exactly the way they did it in the movies. I stepped smartly, trying to figure out who I should copy.

"Any special direction?"

"No," I said. "Anywhere." Last week we had lunch together at Lindell's Vegetarian—but Smyrna had been along. Basically, this was the first time we had gone anywhere alone.

"And were you reading about your favorite subject?"

"Yes," I said. "Magic." He already knew about that. I didn't know what he thought, though. Maybe he thought it was an interest—like wanting to know about rockets or the weather.

He nodded. "I doubt if I have ever met anyone who knew about magic."

"Really," I said. "I have a repertoire."

"A repertoire?"

"Tricks," I said and turned around, walking backward to face him. "Illusions that I perform—I'm quite good. That's not bragging—I'm good."

"You'll show me sometime?"

"Sure," I said and turned back to walk next to him again.

"Did you teach yourself?"

"Yes," I said. This, I realized, was a conversation. Smyrna and I talked to each other, but not like a conversation. "Except my first tricks—I learned them from a magician named Jim Haw the Great."

"Jim Haw?" Theodore had this low voice, almost a whisper.

"When I was a kid," I said. "Very little. Maybe five. I went to this Easter show at the union hall. I don't know if you have ever been to one of those?"

Theodore shook his head.

"Well," I said, "they are alike—usually the singer, whose voice is almost gone, some dumb juggler, and then maybe a comic or a magician. No one with class. This Easter show went a little heavy on the money—they even had a guy dressed in a bunny suit for the last number. But before that they had a magician— Jim Haw the Great. He must have been down on his luck. Out came this man wearing a ratty sweater—no costume. He had a hoarse voice. Then, easy as pie, he was doing the big stuff—cups and balls like I have never seen since. The Japanese version—it was terrific! Pepper's Ghost! Jim Haw was too good to be there. I didn't know anything then, but now—even now—I realize that man was a magician. Well, afterward the performers come out, and the kids got baskets of jelly beans. People crowded around the rabbit, the singer with the spangles—but the magician was alone. I went right up to him. I told him he was the greatest. I asked him to show me only one trick—the disappearing coin. Just that. He sat me right down—there in the front of the auditorium. He took my hands. Yes, he said, you have the hands."

I saw Jim Haw again, as if he were on that street. I had since learned some of his tricks, but he had them down cold—he was perfection. I could actually feel his hug, the rough sweater, the breath of whiskey and tobacco. So long, kid, he said. Good luck.

"I look forward to seeing you perform," Theodore said.

"Sure," I said. I had always thought that if we had ever stayed in one place I could have gotten a few shows. I remembered a girl, Patsy, who tap-danced. She did a lot of the local stuff— American Legion, Knights of Columbus. I could have joined her.

"Rae," Theodore said.

"Yes, Theodore," I said. I was supposed to call him that—no mister. That wasn't hard—I called Smyrna by her first name, and Nat by his most of the time. Sometimes poppo or dad or poppy.

"Do you understand all this, Rae?"

I was tempted to say, All what? But Smyrna had warned me about being a smart aleck.

"I think so," I said.

"Then on Wednesday," Theodore said, "we'll have a ceremony."

"Right."

"The next day is when we will go to Detroit."

I knew the dates—I was counting on the dates.

"On Thursday afternoon—we go to Detroit."

He nodded. "That's right. I have to finish up here—won't be long. We should leave by one o'clock."

I knew the rest of the tale. We would go to his parents' house. We would live there—must be a damn hotel. Two other brothers lived there with their wives, and one sister and her husband. Only Esher down the block lived elsewhere. One big happy family! Everyone ate together. I would have a lot of company, Theodore said. He had a photograph—a row of people, all smiling. Children—seven, eight kids. I imagined myself in that row—fading between Betsy and Toby and Rikla.

I looked up at Theodore. His expression was pleasant. I had never seen him any other way. Good temper. But you can never tell. Smyrna always said, When the door is closed—who knew?

"Rae, I would like to buy you something—it's a tradition. What would you like?"

I knew what he meant—he was thinking ice cream or a soda. He did give me an opening. I planned what I would tell Smyrna. How I didn't wheedle or anything like that. Listen, the man said he wanted to buy me something. I turned left and he followed. I headed toward Hudson's. Hudson's was a classy-looking store.

"That," I said. I used the voice of innocence. I pointed at the window where a mannequin, waving her hand at the admiring crowd of two, wore a pleated skirt, a red-and-blue plaid. I really coveted that skirt. He said he wanted to buy me something. "That skirt."

The slightest shadow grazed Theodore's face. A sixteenth-second frown. But, as I said, I was quick—a magician observes. The frown had almost simultaneous appearance and erasure. Theodore was cool.

"Certainly," he said. "Shall we go in?"

I told the saleswoman. "That skirt in the window, please?"

Oh yes, she had it in my size. Theodore sat down on a chair outside the dressing room. I didn't dawdle in the dressing room. I came out wearing the skirt. Deliberately, I twirled in front of him—the wool twisted around my legs until the extravagance of pleats fell free.

"She looks lovely," the saleswoman said. She avoided saying your daughter—it could be a niece. Sometimes, it probably even turned out to be a sister.

"Yes, she does. Do you like it?"

I gave Theodore a look I had practiced. A beatitude of yearning. "Do I? Does the moon come out at night? I love it!"

"It's yours then."

"Don't wrap it," I said to the saleswoman. The exact intonation used by Joan Crawford. "Don't wrap it," Joan's voice said. "I'll wear it." It wouldn't occur to Theodore to say no. Smyrna would never have allowed such a thing. New belonged in a bag.

The saleswoman followed me into the dressing room and cut off the tags. I wished I had the nerve to tell her to throw away my blue skirt. She took that away to wrap. What would Theodore say when he found out how much the skirt cost? Hudson's wasn't cut-rate. Well, you had to take your chances.

The skirt did a lot for my spirits. I told Theodore all sorts of things on the way back to the apartment—about magic, about girls from my last school—and as often as possible I caught sight of my reflection in store windows.

When we reached my building, I made a gesture. Truly spontaneous, the skirt touching my legs, I leaned forward—tiptoe was not necessary. After all, Theodore had bought me the skirt. One hand balancing against his chest, I was about to kiss him. Oh, the most pristine, the most childish of kisses. My lips were poised to land squarely on Theodore's cheek. Quite the equivalent of the written, Thank you for the Xmas present.

But in one second my benefactor had stepped back, leaving my lips to smack tastelessly against the warmest breeze. Now, he had never touched me—except on the arm. No fondling, no kitchy-kitchy-coo.

"Good-bye," Theodore said. He looked up. Did he spy Smyrna peeking behind a shade? No, his dreamy gaze told me that he saw no one.

The skirt was less an ordeal than I would have expected. A brief exchange of Smyrna's you-asked-for-it versus my he-asked-me-what-I-wanted. All of a sudden Smyrna stopped. For Smyrna, she looked pale. I thought maybe she was sick.

"It's set for Wednesday," she said.

"Yeah—he told me." I dropped the bag with the navy-blue skirt on the floor.

"Listen, Rae," Smyrna said, "he seems all right, doesn't he?"

"He's all right." I smoothed the skirt. "He's giving you cash?" I asked. We had discussed that before. I voted that no checks be exchanged.

Smyrna nodded. "He said cash would be all right."

There were circumstances where I might have felt a little bad about what was about to happen. Theodore wasn't all terrible— nor that hard to take. But I thought of Houdini and The Substitute Trunk Mystery. Manacled and placed trunk inside trunk— still, he got free. Once he was even dropped into the icy Detroit River. I bet they thought of a hundred ways to handcuff him, but he always escaped. What was the principle? What you had to get out of, you had to get out of.

Theodore had plans that made Smyrna nervous. For instance, the wedding. But like I said, I wasn't her kid. Anyway, Smyrna and my prince had gone through the legal formalities. There was a license—blood tests. Papers had mysteriously appeared attesting to the fact that one Raemunde Howard, age seventeen, with the consent of her mother, was to be married. And Smyrna as a bogus me went through all that.

That was what was spooky. I mean, the blood wasn't mine. Nor the shaky handwriting. Don't ask, Smyrna advised. Theodore said that I had to fast on Wednesday—the wedding. No food. What I did was look in the mirror, tried sweeping my hair up, slipped on Smyrna's black pumps. My passion. I tried out a voice. "It's me," I said to an unseen servant. "Yes, it's me. Mrs. Theodore Wilson Fine."

Before anything happened, before I bewitched myself, I dropped the hair and flopped belly down on the bed and pulled out the book—opened to the photograph. Nothing had changed. The girl was still there—standing there with the three babies, not smiling. So much for Mrs. Theodore Wilson Fine.

Smyrna used to say that her wedding stunk. She should have tried mine. I didn't even get a new dress. Smyrna pinned in her white one. Even so, I was less in the chest and more in the hips. No lipstick, hair hanging down. I thought I looked awful. Especially since Smyrna would cry and sob, Oh, God. Then I would cry. We hugged each other. She swore it wasn't going to be bad. Theodore had given her an envelope with the money in hundreds. We counted it twice, although I was positive he wouldn't cheat her. Smyrna went to the bank with one bill and had it changed into tens—it was real.

I didn't get scared until Wednesday. Maybe it was the complexity of the arrangements, or maybe the thrill of marriage had made my flesh sticky. Smyrna had me brush my teeth twice so they wouldn't know I had toast and jelly and milk. She thought the empty-stomach theory was crazy. But around noon I started getting homesick. I realized that Smyrna was not going to the ceremony. I would be there virtually alone.

We started crying again, weeping on each other's shoulders. I felt a strange weakness, a desolation. Then I stopped crying. Smyrna made some ice water, and I rubbed it across my face. This was it—this was marriage.

Right on time, I was picked up by Theodore. We were going in his brother-in-law's black Buick. Esher's husband drove—he said nothing, could have been a hired chauffeur. His wife talked enough for two. Except today—she was a concert of sighs, gave me looks of contempt. She wore what was probably her best dress, a bilious yellow. Her husband sat alone in the front, and I was squeezed between Theodore and Esher like a cushion. Once when the car turned a corner too quickly, I slid against Theodore, touched his hand. Like ice.

We were going to a rabbi's study off Devon Avenue, maybe it was on Kedzie—the bridegroom, me, and a pocket full of phony papers. We parked on a crowded street, uglier than the one we came from. Esher frowned. "Wait." She reached into her purse, pulled out a silver tube. In a second, she had my chin and painted a slash of coral on my lips. I thought I tasted her in the lipstick—saved rancid fat.

I would have rubbed the color off, but too late. The festive party tumbled from car to sidewalk.

The rabbi had been skillfully chosen—ancient man, his eyes magnified behind thick lenses. I could have been anyone. His wife was a diminutive person, her wig askew, her body a concentration of calcium.

I realized that I had never been to a wedding before. Really—never. This one took maybe fifteen minutes. I signed something, Theodore signed something. The old woman called me the *kalleh*. Esher kissed the air near my cheek. Her eyes said mistake, mistake, mistake.

Somehow I thought we would go home—rather, I would go home. The car would stop, I would shake hands with Theodore, I was even willing to kiss my new in-laws, and then, with a jolly good-bye, I'd go up the stairs, open the front door. And Smyrna would give me supper.

That's how much the bride was willing. Instead, Esher's husband left us off at the door—not my door—while he went to park. Esher was now heaving her discontent. Her pot roast was cold. Theodore was matter-of-fact. What I did was close my eyes very tightly and concentrate. It was easy. You focus. I focused on that photograph—the girl, unsmiling, the small crowd of her children.

"We'll leave for Detroit tomorrow," Theodore said. We were inside Esher's apartment; we were in the hall; he was taking off his jacket, hanging it up. So he did take *it* off.

"Right," I said. What was polite? Should I offer to help in the kitchen? Theodore, the bridegroom, sat down in the living room, unfolded the newspaper. The *kalleh* trotted into the kitchen. How had Esher gotten out of the yellow dress so quickly? Now wrapped in slightly soiled green, she rummaged in the refrigerator.

"Can I help?"

She stared. "Set the table." Pointed to a cabinet—inside, porridge-colored dishes, sooty glasses. Nothing like a family dinner. It was when I was setting the table that I saw my suitcase in the hall. That was eerie. I knew the contents—I had packed it. My life in a suitcase. It was Smyrna's best case, that one. No one can pack a suitcase the way I can. From a book, I learned a magician's trick with scarves and applied that technique to folding. Nothing ever wrinkled.

I put the plates on the table with unadorned hands. Theodore had already taken back the gold ring. I would wear it when we reached Detroit, he said. I didn't like it anyway. Plain. At that time I had no taste for plain.

We had pot roast. Esher served huge bowls of mushroom and barley soup with great ovoid globes of yellow fat skating across the surface. I thought it would have been great to celebrate with champagne. None of that. At the end of the meal, Esher started to pour coffee. Yes, please, I said. Esher looked at Theodore. He must have nodded, permission given. I got a cup.

After dinner I helped with the dishes, but nothing I did endeared me to the pink pig, and vice versa. Then we had a happy two hours of what they wanted to watch. I was dying for a book— but hell wouldn't have gotten me near that suitcase.

Esher's apartment wasn't rented furnished. Only two blocks away from where Smyrna and I had lived and people had their own furniture. I didn't think much of my sister-in-law's possessions. Too much. How could you run a Hoover past all that stuff?

Esher and Mister Silent had two bedrooms, but one was like a television room or something. Fortunately, there were no little Eshers.

But then, boom. It was lights out. The sleeping arrangements. The newly married couple apparently were to occupy the bedroom. Esher and hubby were going across the hall to stay with some old lady. Giving her a cock-and-bull story that I would have loved to hear.

I thought someone was going to tell me to do something—take a bath or brush your teeth. There were no instructions. I stood like a statue—pretended to be a statue in the middle of that room. The room was buried in wood. A three-drawer chest, a six-drawer chest. Two night tables. A chair. Also, lamps with pink shades under cellophane wrappers. A rug of roses. A large bed minus a bedspread. All the wood was dark—nothing cheery about these people.

I heard the door close, cutting off the obvious annoyance of Esher *en famille.* Theodore, my shirt-sleeved Theodore, carried in my suitcase. It was obvious. I was staying.

"Get undressed, Rae," he said.

He left the room, closed the bedroom door. I lifted the suitcase onto the bed. Smyrna had a surprise on top of my clothes. A nightgown. I had never owned a nightgown before. It was obviously new—the label stiff and scratchy to the touch. I dug down. What had she done! Where were my pajamas? My wonderful, my worn, my own pajamas. They were gone.

I hung up Smyrna's borrowed white dress. Then I took it off the hanger, pinched the pins closed, taking care to snag the material, rolled it into a ball, and stuffed it in the corner of the closet between shoe boxes and a pile of cedar chips.

Reluctantly, I slipped on the nightgown over my undershirt and my underpants. Strength, I decided, was in layers. I got into bed. I had almost fallen asleep—the day had been long—when Theodore came back into the room. He turned off the lights—no, he left on one lamp. My back was to him. Would he understand?

I felt him get into the bed, a sudden draft as the sheet lifted. Then I felt his hands, I was being turned around. We started to kiss, real kisses, on my cheeks, my chin, my lips. Miss Cloakroom with true experience had once told me that that part you shouldn't worry about. When they start pulling up the dress—watch out. His hands were pushing up the nightgown—Smyrna's choice—fondling my chest beneath the undershirt. Very well, I shoved him hard, knees up. He opened his eyes—looked as if he couldn't believe it. We weren't talking. But my knees had hit bare skin. My bridegroom was bare. We had this uneven wrestling match. Still, I could keep my knees clenched even when I wriggled around. His tongue had turned warm. I could hear his breathing. He had my gown, the hell with the gown. The lace edge ripped off in scalloped strips. The straps of my undershirt bound my arms. That hurt. I kicked him in the belly. I fought for the underpants. He kept crashing down on top of me. I yelled, Stop! You ass!

He never made a real sound—breathing wasn't exactly noise.

I pulled away—he leaped for my ankles, missed, and tumbled to the floor. My turn! I twirled around. Hadn't I trained myself to look carefully, be observant? On Esher's dresser, a mirrored tray holding a collection of unopened perfume bottles. I grabbed the carved handle of that tray, raised it, and smacked it down across the bridegroom's head, just now rising from the floor. The tray made a whack sound, and Theodore, with one short wheezing hum, lay still. Two bottles of perfume had cracked into a pile of glass icicles on the dresser, creating a network of tiny canals as varnish dissolved.

I was exhausted. There was a clock on one night table—miraculously still intact. Twelve midnight. I certainly wasn't going to leave until morning. I crawled back on the bed, pulled the sheet over me, and fell into an exhausted and complete sleep.

———

I didn't wake up until it was light—the sun coming like pin-pricks through Esher's stupid curtains. Then I realized what woke me. Theodore's body suspended above mine, my legs opened by his knees, as I did what the girls swore was the act of Miss Cloak-room. I was only half awake; he had pinned both my wrists with one of his hands. I carried suddenly his full weight.

"Oh God," Theodore whispered—although probably not to me—"I am ruined, I am ruined."

I fell asleep again. When I woke up, he was gone. I had to look at the room to believe that the night had happened. The lamps were broken, although I didn't remember that part. I heard the argument through the door. Esher screaming. I was a devil, I was Golem, I had killed her—yes, killed her. Well, I couldn't blame her. The room was a mess. On the other hand, I didn't like the idea of her peeking in when I had been asleep.

I could hardly hear Theodore's replies to his sister's accusations. But he was apparently paying her. And the way she shut up, it must have been more than the destruction was worth.

In two seconds he was in the room. I hesitated, but then I decided not to pretend to be asleep.

"Good morning, Rae," he said.

I looked at him. Black suit in place. A hideous bruise across one cheek. I almost felt sorry. But sorry kept you locked in a trunk. What was I thinking about? Houdini. He was always pre-pared. No matter how ingenious the locks, how crafty the design of the handcuffs, he always emerged triumphant. So forget senti-ments of surrender. I also had devised a scheme, an itinerary for escape. But I had to be careful. Never underestimate the audi-ence. One slip and my plan would go down the drain.

"Good morning," I said. I'll give him that—he didn't even glance in the direction of last night's battle. The tray reflected sparkles upward from the rug.

"By noon I'll be back. We'll start for home then."

Now that froze my bones. Home!

"Sure," I said. I thought he stared too sharply then. I mustn't sound like too amiable an idiot. So I stared back—just a touch of belligerence. That seemed to satisfy him.

"Watch her," I heard him say to Esher before he left the apartment.

I got dressed. I put on the plaid skirt, white blouse. I figured I deserved that skirt. I took nothing. I knew that would give me away—carry one thing and arouse suspicion.

No, I didn't want any breakfast. Esher shrugged. What did she care.

"I'm going to say good-bye to Smyrna," I said.

"What?" She turned around.

I didn't hesitate—it was the moment for a tantrum, if necessary. But first I tried plain annoyance. "I want to say good-bye—what's wrong with that!"

Esher looked at me. Clearly, watching me didn't suit her. She had better things to do. And I carried nothing, nothing. I knew what she thought—her brother had made a mistake. Right.

What happened afterward wasn't Smyrna's fault. She was innocent. She made the contract in good faith. Yes, I had a plan. I never told Smyrna. She never knew. So she was not to blame in any way.

Slowly, oh, so slowly, I left. This was the point where the plan could go in lots of directions. I had considered who I knew in the neighborhood. Forget the gaggle of women that Smyrna talked to—they would assume I was cuckoo. The librarians were possibilities. But high on the list was Porcelana. She might be weird, but she wasn't stupid.

I walked first to our building. I knew that was dumb—there wasn't a lot of time. Smyrna was supposed to leave yesterday, fast. But who knew, maybe she was still here. I had my key. As soon as I turned the lock, I knew she had gone.

This was my smart-aleck period. I was certain of everything. Like, for instance, that Porcelana would be home. I walked up the stairs and knocked. She was home.

"Can't play," she said, annoyed. "I'm going shopping. Come back later."

"I need advice," I said.

She glared.

"Advice?"

"Yes."

Now, I looked up straight into her eyes.

"Can a girl my age get married?"

"What?"

"I'm eleven. I don't know anyone to ask."

"Married! Why the hell would you get married? Who told you that? Where is what's-her-name? That woman?"

"Gone. I was married yesterday—I think."

"You were what?"

That was it. And by and large my smart-aleck period ended. I entered Child Welfare. I was asked about family. Smyrna, whom I claimed as a cousin, had gone to Canada, I said. I owed her that.

What I did have were a few names. The papers had all left with Smyrna. I had memorized what was useful. I gave Child Welfare the name of Minnie Howard. Grandmother Minnie Howard. I never intended to spend my life as a floater. This was close to, but not quite at the end of, my smart-aleck period, so I also wrote to Minnie Howard myself. I assumed she lacked a heart of gold— but, nevertheless, I outlined my plight. Including the marriage. I hoped—and added the possibility of praying—that I might come and live with her. Barring that, I suggested, well, unless I heard from her, I would write similar letters to other members of the family. Didn't she have three sisters? I would tell them everything—including the marriage.

When I left Child Welfare, I rode all the way from Chicago to New York by train. I think the woman who picked me up knew the entire story, because she stared at me the whole time we rode uptown to Washington Heights.

I was nervous. I was about to meet my grandmother and I had never seen her before. At least not that I remembered. I had my ideas about where I was going to live—Smyrna said Minnie Howard was a Queen Bee. A woman in a white uniform opened the door. She was a practical nurse. The woman from social services went in first. I stayed in the living room. I was in shock—I had not expected this. The place looked as if Esher had furnished it.

I cleared my throat. "Is she very sick?"

The nurse looked at me. "She's a pain in the ass," she said.

The woman from social services finally came out. She gave me a short and uncomforting hug. I was to be a good girl, she said. I would be fine. Now, I was to go in—I could introduce myself.

Minnie Howard lay in a bed, a large mahogany bed. Two night tables clung to its edges. A chest, a dresser. A chair.

She wasn't as old as I had expected. She was almost sitting, a pile of pillows behind her back.

"Hello," I said. Then, in case she was uncertain. "I'm Rae."

"I know who you are. Well, come over by the bed—unless you expect me to dance over to you. If this doesn't work out, young lady, you are going right back."

I nodded. But right back to where? I leaned over, hands carefully in view, and extracted a quarter from behind her ear.

"See," I said, smiling.

"That's mine," Minnie Howard said. "You little thief!"

I spent the next eight years of my life with Minnie Howard. I met the rest of the family two months later at a dinner—a pot-luck party.

Two cousins caught me in the back hall that first day, blocked my way. Their eyes glittered with malice and hope. "Is it true?" one of them asked. "Did you do *it?*"

As I said, my time as a smart aleck was over. And my first marriage had come and gone. "He never touched me," I said. "Never laid a hand on me." They didn't know what I was talking about, then someone called us. It was time to eat.

Conjuring—the doing of magic—came to me when I was very young. I learned that behind every trick, every illusion was the explanation. And knowing that made me a realist at an early age. Still, the first time I heard someone call out "Miz Magic," I felt as if my identity had suddenly appeared. Yes, yes—that was me. Presenting Miz Magic. It's Miz Magic. Ah, Miz Magic. Who you are can occur at any time.